A FABLE ABOUT LIVING
YOUR 4TH QUARTER INTENTIONALLY

no regrets

ALLEN HUNT &
MATTHEW KELLY

wellspring

"Art is a spiritual pursuit
It is wrestling with the angels
It is dancing with the gods"
From *Dancing With the Gods*
by Kent Nerburn
Copyright © 2018 by Kent Nerburn

ISBN: 978-1-63582-266-3 (hardcover)

Designed by Ashley Dias

10   9   8   7   6   5   4   3   2   1

FIRST EDITION

Printed in the United States of America

With gratitude to
Dynamic Catholic Ambassadors
for sharing in this great mission

table of contents

Remember that you are dust
and to dust you shall return.

GENESIS 3:19

part one

THE ACCIDENT

"We all are [on our way out];
act accordingly."

— Jack Nicholson in *The Departed*

I. THE ACCIDENT

It wasn't raining, but it looked like it would start at any second.

Lisa Larson drove home from work on Monday after a long day of showing houses to a client. Another couple moving to Nashville from Los Angeles.

She tuned her radio to the local traffic report and heard the all too familiar announcement of a gruesome accident on the interstate between Cool Springs and Brentwood. Lisa loved Nashville, but the growth clogging the roads had sparked her to think it just might not be her forever place.

She quickly realized she was heading directly toward the location of the multi-car pileup.

Lisa didn't worry too much about it. Traffic defined much of her day now as a real estate agent scurrying between neighborhoods in the suburbs.

Plus, worry just wasn't her style. Although since the death of her husband, Brian, eight years ago, she did find herself fretting more now than the younger Lisa ever would have. But traffic would not get her down. Money issues, maybe. A few pounds gained, probably. But certainly not traffic.

Music soon returned to her speakers. And she began to look for the next exit to get off the freeway and find a way home on the back roads. Traffic delays were such a hassle, but she knew how to navigate them well.

A mile passed, but there were no exits. Lisa fidgeted a bit because she wasn't sure how much longer she had before she would reach the wreck. She really did not want to sit on the highway for an hour waiting for an accident to be cleared. She had other things to do. Like preparing dinner, for starters.

She looked around and noticed other drivers hearing the news about the pileup of vehicles ahead. Their concerned faces showed the same worry about wasted time in a lengthy delay on the afternoon commute.

Traffic slowed from its normal pace of seventy miles per hour. She didn't see any brake lights ahead, so she knew she still had a few more minutes to find a way off the interstate.

Another traffic report emerged from the radio. Lisa turned up the volume and focused intently on the reporter's words as if they emanated from the Oracle of Delphi. She noticed the helicopters hovering above the road in the distance just ahead. She knew what that meant. An hour, maybe more, going nowhere while police, medics, and tow trucks cleared the road and evacuated any injured people. And probably a fast food drive-through dinner in a sack rather than going home and preparing something healthier for herself.

Her cell phone rang. She recognized the number: her youngest child, Christopher. He usually worked late at the software firm where he had landed after college. He liked to call her in the early evening just to check in. She smiled and gave thanks for her thoughtful twenty-eight-year-old baby boy. But she knew she needed to focus on the traffic report and the congestion building around her. So she let Christopher's call go to voicemail.

In front of her, brake lights lit up like a pinball machine. Cars slowed and she could see that the traffic had come to a complete stop just ahead.

Still no exits to be found. The traffic reporter was warning drivers to get off the road to alternate routes.

Her phone rang again. Christopher. Again.

But Lisa wanted to stay focused, so she let the call go to voicemail. Again.

She could see an exit ramp just ahead. Her last chance! Just two lanes over to the right and she could get off on that ramp. She thought she could squeeze in. She darted over into the next lane.

Her side mirror's blind spot caused her eye to miss a white van occupying that space one lane over. Before she even realized it, her car began to spin. She no longer had control. Her vehicle careened into the front of a large truck. Too many cars and nowhere for the truck driver to go. An 18-wheeler.

All went dark.

In an instant, Lisa finds herself hovering above her home parish. Sacred Heart Catholic Church. A place where she has attended Mass hundreds of times over the years. Her spiritual home.

The pews are populated with a small group of people. Thirty-five or forty at most.

A coffin rests near the front of the church, beside the altar.

A handful of flower bouquets stand arranged next to the coffin.

The priest proceeds down the center aisle, followed by a cluster of people. All wearing black.

Lisa looks down carefully from the rafters at the procession below. She quickly identifies the people behind the priest: her own family members.

Her firstborn son, Michael, and his wife, Susan, pregnant with their first child.

Her daughter, Emily, and her husband, Ron, carrying their newborn son, Noah. Lisa's first grandchild.

Following behind, Christopher.

Trailing them, Lisa's four siblings, their spouses, and most of her nieces and nephews make their way toward the pews reserved for family.

Suddenly Lisa realizes: "This is your own funeral, bucko. What the heck? That's your body lying in the casket. How can this be? You're actually attending your own funeral."

Her mind races frantically. Are those really the clothes her children picked out for her? Didn't they know she wanted to be cremated? That she had purchased an urn so she could be placed next to Brian in the columbarium here at the parish? What's the matter with them?!

In the front pews sit a few of her closest friends. The sparse crowd surprises Lisa.

"It must be a workday," she thinks. "Or perhaps there's bad weather."

She cherishes a number of friends who she knows would be here if it were at all possible. But they are not present on this day.

Lisa remembers the first funeral she went to when she was a child. It didn't feel much like this one. That's for sure. It seemed to have more, well, life to it. Energy. Enthusiasm. A joy for the person who had died.

It was her grandmother who had passed away then. And Lisa remembers being there with her four siblings, all her cousins, and her whole extended family, giving thanks for her grandmother's life and laughing at the way she used to mispronounce the name of her own hometown in Illinois.

This group at Sacred Heart today shares no joy or laughter. They wear the blank soldier-like faces of people simply doing their duty.

As the Mass concludes (thanks be to God, her children remembered how much she loves the beauty of a funeral Mass), the priest invites Christopher up to speak on behalf of the family.

Christopher thanks everyone for coming today.

"It's a hard day to bury a parent," he says. "But there's probably no such thing as an easy day to do that.

"Especially a parent who dies too soon. Without any warning. One day, at work. A normal day. But then, a traffic accident. A wreck that changes everything in an instant. There was no time to prepare for Mom's death. And now we can't go back."

Christopher shares how he loved his mother. He gives thanks for her.

He pauses.

Then he chuckles and says, "Do all parents think they are a nine or a ten? Is that a thing? When really they are just a five or maybe a six?"

"What in the world is he saying?" Lisa exclaims to herself. "Doesn't he know he's supposed to say really nice things about me at my funeral?"

Instead, Christopher is speaking simply and honestly. Just telling the truth.

He describes how Lisa thought she was really there for him and was always reminding him how much she loved him. But that her actions often failed to support her words.

He shares how her presence and attention were hit-or-miss. That at times he felt invisible around her. She just had so much going on—with work, and friends, and gardening, and all that. She tried; she really did. But when he really needed to talk, she didn't seem able to pay deep attention and listen.

Christopher mentions how Lisa frequently liked to say, "I'm the most generous person I know."

He says he hopes that was true, but that he remembers very few instances of her actually giving money to her parish or to help other people. But he knows it was important to her. After all, she said it all the time, and he hopes there were examples he just doesn't know about. He tells the group how Lisa certainly was not cheap or stingy, just probably very average.

"Like so many of us. Again, maybe a five or a six on a scale of one to ten," he says.

Lisa watches from above as Christopher finishes his "eulogy."

And she wonders if she really was who she wanted to be? Was she, well, just so ... average? Merely OK as a parent? Always a little distracted. Not particularly generous. Did her life somehow miss the mark?

She doesn't think about what she wishes Christopher had said. No, really, she thinks about what she hopes was *actually true*. About her. And about her life.

Lisa certainly never set out to be average. As a girl, she had high expectations. She dreamed of becoming an artist. Of being a great mom. She certainly never intended to do just enough to get by.

After all, no one ever intends to be too busy to really care about other people, especially the people you love the most.

She looks around the church and notices all the things that will carry on without her. The priest. The Mass. The beautiful stained glass.

She always meant to donate funds to help replace the one broken out by a kid throwing rocks at the church one night. But it's still patched up, waiting for repair or replacement. Lisa meant well. But she never quite got around to it. Maybe Christopher had a point.

She gazes at her son. His words surprised. And

stung. Lisa really does love him. Now she wonders if she somehow under-delivered that love to him.

She shifts her eyes to her daughter. Emily is so beautiful. In a profound way Lisa really did not notice before. She exudes that soft glow of a new mother. Lisa prays to God that Emily and her husband will have more grandchildren. And that Emily will have kind things to tell those children about their grandmother and the qualities they inherited from her. A grandmother gone too soon.

Lisa thinks about her husband. A tinge of disappointment brushes her heart. Her marriage had started with great love. And big dreams. But somehow, as the years set in, that love had cooled. And the dreams fell by the wayside in the mundane routine of daily life: going to work, raising the kids, and trying to find just a little time for yourself.

Did they thrive or did they merely survive? Brian died so suddenly. At the age of fifty-two. And it was over. Just like that.

Lisa notices the flowers. So beautiful.

The music plays on. "Love Divine." She always did love that song. So inspiring.

The priest leads the people out of the church.

Now Lisa is alone. Hovering above. Looking down on what was.

Her parish. Her friends. Her family. Her life.

Their lives, this world, will go on.

Lisa will not.

"You have died," she says to herself.

"You wish you had time to prepare. But you didn't. It was all so sudden.

"And now you are gone."

part two

THE STRUGGLE

"People may spend their whole lives climbing the ladder of success only to find, once they reach the top, that the ladder is leaning against the wrong wall."

— Thomas Merton

II. AWAKENING

The alarm rings—blares, really. Jarring Lisa from her sleep.

She is not a morning person.

Lying in bed, she realizes it's Tuesday. A new day. Slowly, she stumbles like Lazarus out of the dark cave of sleep into the light of day.

Then Lisa realizes.

It must have been a dream.

Asleep then, awake now.

Dark then, daylight now.

At her own funeral then. Lying here in her bed now.

It was just a dream.

Wow.

She's not at her funeral after all. Rather, she's in her own bed in Nashville on a Tuesday morning. Just a Tuesday. Nothing extraordinary about it. A normal day of clients waiting to be shown houses.

The dream was so real. The funeral so specific and emotional. Now she has stepped from death back into her life.

Lisa's mind fog gradually burns off. Her eyes gaze out the window at the roses in her backyard. They're still there. This really is Tuesday. And this really is still her home. And her bed.

But the details of the dream don't slip away. The car wreck. The darkness. The parish. The funeral Mass. But most of all, the words of her son remain with her.

Is she just that average? Is her life really that lackluster?

A single thought races around her mind like a hamster: "You are going to die."

Not a very uplifting idea. But still true.

She knows she's going to die. We all know that. Brian had died eight years ago. Ever since then, she's known even more that she will die too.

But somehow, now it's real. Not an idea out there somewhere. Instead, a reality staring her squarely in the face.

The dream has stunned her.

"You will be dead soon," she thinks. "It could even happen today."

So Lisa lies in bed and lets her mind wander into neighborhoods it has not visited before:

Have I really experienced the beauty of life?

Have I even come close to becoming the-best-ver-sion-of-myself?

Have I really even given it a try?

Have I contributed something, anything, meaning-ful to the world?

Have I lived?

Have I loved?

Do I matter?

Lisa realizes she's been issued a rare warning that few people ever receive. Like the arrival of a messenger pigeon from heaven. Most of us simply are alive one minute, then dead the next.

But a clear message has been delivered. And now Lisa needs to let it marinate.

Knowing death is not far off brings clarity.

Once you receive that news, there's no middle ground: something is either very important or it's not important at all.

Regrets flood Lisa's mind. Arriving so fast she can barely process them:

- I wish I'd had the courage to just be myself.
- I wish I had spent more time with the people I love.
- I wish I had made spirituality more of a priority.
- I wish I had discovered my purpose earlier.
- I wish I had learned to express my feelings more.
- I wish I hadn't spent so much time worrying about things that never happened.
- I wish I had taken more risks.
- I wish I had cared less about what other people thought.
- I wish I had taken better care of myself.
- I wish I had been a better wife.
- I wish I hadn't spent so much time chasing the wrong things.
- I wish I'd had more children.
- I wish I had thought about life's big questions earlier.
- I wish I had pursued more of my dreams.

Even though Brian died, Lisa realizes she really has never thought much about death—and certainly not about her own.

Here she is, fifty-nine years old, about to turn sixty. Lying in bed on a Tuesday morning. So overwhelmed by the thought of death that she has no inclination whatsoever to get up, get dressed, and get on with her day. Suddenly, showing houses to people relocating to Tennessee just doesn't seem all that important.

Lisa arrives at a startling conclusion: "My life is not what I wanted it to be."

She's not completely sure what she wanted from life, but she knows it's certainly not to have her precious Christopher get up at her funeral Mass and say she was merely OK as a mom and as a person. What in the world does that mean?

"In fact, what does this dream mean?" she asks.

Lisa knows she needs to keep it to herself. If she tells her friends, or even her family, about this dream, they'll only laugh and shrug it off. Tell her to get back to her life. Say it was just a dream.

But she senses something larger going on here.

At the very least, she's about to turn sixty. And Lisa knows now she wants to live the rest of her life with no regrets.

III. FRIENDS

Lisa, Jen, and Amy had made plans to meet for lunch at the Bistro. At the table they always gathered around. The one tucked into the front window where you could watch the whole world walk by on the street slightly beneath you. A cozy place to sit and enjoy a glass of wine.

The three friends called themselves "the Wine Girls." And liked to joke that maybe their nickname really should be "the Whine Girls." Because they liked to meet for a glass of wine and to whine a little too.

The Wine Girls had known each other for more years than they could count. Ever since they had lived in the same neighborhood when their kids were just little tikes. The moms, and the kids, had grown up together.

Today, Lisa had a chunk of free time in the middle of her day, so she was happy to catch up with Jen and Amy for a leisurely lunch. And a glass of Chardonnay.

That dream still bounced inside her head. So much so that she just wanted to forget about it for a little while and feel normal again. What better way to do that than with a little wine and some whine?

Jen arrived first. She always did. She grabbed the coveted table in the front window and ordered a glass of water. A tennis match awaited her later that afternoon. Slender, athletic and tan, Jen liked to be active and outdoors any chance she got. The only thing she loved more than tennis was the beach.

Having grown up in Nashville, she had watched the city relentlessly expand all around her. But she still amazed her friends with how many people she seemed to know anywhere she went. Today was no exception. When Lisa arrived, she found Jen talking to the waitress. Jen had dated the young woman's father decades ago, before she had met her husband, Kevin. A lawyer like Jen's father had been, Kevin remained strikingly handsome. Jen and Kevin stood out wherever they went. And Jen liked that.

Lisa removed the sunglasses resting in her wavy brown hair, sat down and ordered the glass of Chardonnay she'd been anticipating. Always wrestling with the challenges of menopausal weight gain, she allowed herself the glorious indulgence of a glass or two of wine. She would walk off the calories later that evening in her nightly stroll around the neighborhood.

Lisa smiled as she shared, "I can't wait till tomorrow. The older I get, the more I love Saturdays. In the morning, me and the Saturday Servants will take Communion to homebound parishioners. Shut-ins, nursing home residents, and people in hospice. After that, a free day. Hallelujah!"

Jen nodded and whispered, "I'm concerned about Ashley. She's thirty-three; do you think she'll ever get married? Will I get any grandkids? She's been really distant lately. Secretive. She doesn't say much about anything. I think she may be avoiding me. Do you think she has some kind of eating disorder?"

Just then, Amy arrived. The third in their holy trinity of Wine Girl friendship, Amy too had been looking forward to a glass of wine. She preferred German wines. It was her small way of remembering her only child, Craig, a member of the military, now stationed in Germany.

Amy and her husband, Daniel, had hoped for more children, but those hopes had gone unfulfilled. Perhaps because of that disappointment, she brought a caring spirit to every conversation. Faithful to her friends, she knew well the pain of broken dreams.

The three women enjoyed their casual lunch. And the free conversation that comes with relishing the company of people you have known and trusted for years.

Jen then snuck out early to head to her tennis match. Amy and Lisa lingered for another half hour or so just to savor the pleasure of friendship.

This return to normalcy washed over Lisa with the same warmth the glass of Chardonnay had produced. And she escaped for a moment the haunting vision of her own funeral.

IV. STIRRING

Lisa woke with a start.

Her eyes lingered on the empty side of her bed. Where Brian had slept all those years.

She gazed at his pillow.

In a way, it felt like he had died so long ago that she could barely remember his face. But right now, the eight years that had passed since his death felt like a mere instant.

Lisa struggled to remember the details of her husband's kind face.

When they had met in college, Brian's life overflowed with friends and hangers-on. He had always been so popular. Making friends just came naturally to him. Lisa had simply fit right into the mix.

After college, Brian had started as a trainee at a large telecom firm, then moved into a role in management. He never reached great heights in his job, but his popularity followed him from college into his working life. He always was fun-loving. He never lacked for friends. And his work colleagues seemed to value his presence. Golf. Beer. His car. His friends. He enjoyed all of these more than he did working.

Lisa stepped into a soft mist of memories. At times, it was as if Brian loved all the stuff outside his family more than he did her or the kids. He provided, to be sure. He was faithful. And he was present. But Brian rarely acted like he really wanted to be there.

He had dropped dead in the driveway after a Friday afternoon round of golf. It was just so sudden. No time to say goodbye. Or to prepare. Just gone. Right there in front of the house. At age fifty-two.

Lisa realized the dream of her own death had stirred a residue deep within her she could not quite name yet. Memories, feelings, and dreams all began to bubble within her. Like carbonation in a bottled drink, just waiting for the cap to be popped.

V. THE BIRTHDAY PARTY

When everyone yelled, "*Surprise!*" Lisa nearly wet her pants.

She hadn't expected a party. She had no inkling it was even in the works.

So, as Lisa walked into the Bistro and saw all her children, along with Jen, Amy, and their husbands standing there, she nearly collapsed in shock.

Her sixtieth birthday. And a party to celebrate. Who knew?!

Jen loved to organize. And thoughtful Amy had ensured all the little details were done just right. The two of them really did make the perfect team.

They'd reserved the room in the back. That way, everyone could gather, share a few drinks and tell stories in a private setting.

And tell stories they did.

Michael, Lisa's oldest son, shared his favorite story of the family's vacations in the Florida Panhandle near Destin. The road trip in the van with all the kids.

"Do y'all remember how Mom used to make us

listen to her music? No one else could even make a suggestion. It was all her college music, all the time, all the way to the beach in Destin. Every year. Oh my gosh!"

Everyone laughed.

Lisa's daughter, Emily, had arranged for her newborn boy, Noah, to stay with his other grandparents for the weekend. That way, she and her husband could drive over from Memphis. Lisa didn't express her disappointment that little Noah wouldn't be joining in this party even though he was her first grandchild for heaven's sake. What were they thinking? But she didn't mention it, pleased that everyone cared enough to come celebrate this moment with her.

Christopher, who was still single, told about learning to garden with his mother in the back yard.

"Mom loves eating her own homegrown tomatoes. That's for sure. But what she loves even more than that are those dang roses. Mom loves them more than us."

Everyone smiled and looked at Lisa as she gazed warmly at her Christopher. He was not a little boy anymore, but he still lived in that same place in her heart.

"I'd be running around, poking into thorns. Crying my eyes out. And her eyes would never leave that bush. Trimming an extra leaf here, pruning a random branch there. Focus, I tell you. Complete, undivided focus."

Amy, never one to say much in public, simply raised her glass.

"Here's to a friend, loyal and true. May God bless you and this sixtieth year too!"

Then Jen took the spotlight. Her favorite place. She delighted in moments when all eyes fixed squarely on her.

Her sentimental words surprised everyone.

"Lisa, you're a true friend. Time-tested. Battle-worn. I can't remember how many years we've known each other now, but it's a bunch!"

The party-goers chuckled.

"You've stood faithful and strong through them all. When my son wrecked his bike in the street, you were the first one there. You scooped him up and headed straight to the ER. You didn't even wait for me. Thank you," Jen continued. "When I had my hysterectomy, you sat with me afterward in the hospital. You knew you didn't need to say much. Just being there said it all."

She looked at her husband, Kevin. "By the way, where were you anyway?"

The group laughed as Kevin wiggled, wearing an embarrassed blush.

"I love you and cherish our times together," Jen said to Lisa. "Especially our girls' beach weekend in the fall. That weekend gets written in all caps with exclamation points on my calendar every single year."

Jen, Amy, and Lisa enjoyed an intimate bond largely because of that uninterrupted annual escape. Time just to be honest and real with one another.

"I've fallen away from the Church," Jen shared, "but you have remained steady and faithful. I don't know how. That Father Lawrence drives me crazy. He's just so ... wellll ... OK ... there's no time for that right now."

After a pause, she continued. "Everyone around me seems to be giving up on the faith. But there you were, and there you are, still. That says something about you. I'm not sure what, but it says something."

Now, everyone was at ease. Jen knew how to work a crowd. She stitched the group together with their shared memories. And their shared sufferings.

"As hard as it is for me to admit, I've always looked up to you, Lisa. When Brian died so suddenly, you navigated those choppy waters and cleaned up the mess he left you. And you never said a word. Grace. Pure grace under pressure you showed me. You showed all of us.

"And you haven't quit. Yes, we age. Yes, we all have a few wrinkles we're noticing in the mirror in the morning. And yes, we all cringe at a few pounds we wish weren't popping up ... and out. But you've kept on going without a word of complaint. I'm sure you worry. I'm sure being a widow is more challenging than I can possibly imagine. I admire you. You're a strong woman. Loyal. Caring. And I give thanks for these years of friendship. Maybe even one day your faith will draw me back too. Who knows? Happy sixtieth birthday. You deserve the best of everything!"

The room erupted in a cheer, with one loud "Hip hip hooray!" from Michael.

Dinner arrived. The group sat down and enjoyed an evening of family and hard-earned friendship, won over more than three decades of simply doing life together.

Afterward, Lisa's spirit glowed. She gave thanks. God's goodness abounded in her life. Children. Grand-children. Long-time friends.

"Is there really anything better?" she thought. "Yes, if they had just brought along little Noah!"

One conversation lingered, still ping-ponging around her ears. During drinks, she had spoken with Kevin. A lawyer, Jen's husband tended to be blunt. He also tended to assume everyone cared deeply about what he had to say. Maybe it was because he was so handsome.

As they had chatted, Kevin said, "You're turning sixty, Lisa. Good for you. The average woman lives to be just past eighty. That means you're three-fourths of the way through your life. Twenty years to go. You're starting your fourth quarter."

Her fourth quarter. The final stretch of her life.

She had never thought of life in those terms before.

Lisa's mind returned to her dream. Her own funeral.

Maybe, she thought, God was trying to tell her something.

VI. A DIFFERENT WAY

Still glowing from the night before, Lisa drove to meet Christopher and Emily for lunch.

"If I could paint a picture of my life right now," she said to herself, "it would look like a Thanksgiving cornucopia of blessings."

Lisa longed for some special time with her sweet Emily before she headed back to Memphis. She didn't want to embarrass her own daughter, so she resolved again not to ask why in the world Emily had not brought little Noah to the party.

"I mean, really, who comes to Mimi's sixtieth birthday and doesn't bring the grandson?" she asked herself, shaking her head. "The firstborn. Seriously."

Lisa entered the restaurant parking lot. As the speakers in her car celebrated the songs of her youth, the lyrics penetrated her ear.

It's over before you know it.
It all goes by so fast.
The bad nights take forever,
And the good nights don't ever seem to last.

Again? Really? "I mean, come on, God!" Lisa thought. "You certainly are not being subtle here."

First, the stunning dream of her own funeral. Then, Kevin's provocative fourth quarter comment at her sixtieth birthday party. And now, even the music lilting through her car?

She thought again about Brian's sudden heart attack.

Lisa *really* did not want to live, or die, in the same way her husband had.

First, she didn't want the kids to feel like she had short-changed them for her friends or her hobbies. Brian certainly had loved the kids. They knew that. He just never seemed to be particularly invested in them. There had been no long conversations. No enthusiastic encouragement to do well in school. No prayers said at night over them to entrust them to the bigger Father.

Maybe it was because she was a mom. Lisa just knew: in the end, your relationships will be what matter. She wanted her time with her children and grandchild (with a second on the way soon) to count. For there to be a nest of love built around all her birds. A love to bind them together in a special way. Even after she was gone.

She wasn't sure exactly what that looked like. But she did know that after Brian had died, it wasn't long before no one mentioned him again. Not even his kids. She knew for sure she didn't want that.

More than that, Lisa knew she didn't want to die like Brian. Sudden. Alone. With no real faith to speak of.

Lisa loved her faith deeply. She always had. Growing up in Illinois, she had been immersed in Catholicism. Her mom and dad made sure the family prayed the Rosary together each Saturday night. They hosted the priest for dinner each year around Thanksgiving, so the kids would know him personally and be inspired by his life. And they never allowed their five kids to schedule anything other than Mass and family time on Sundays. No exceptions. Ever.

Lisa realized now that she had not created that same setting for her own children. Her heart dragged the weight of knowing her kids were not as equipped for the ups and downs of life as she herself had been.

She, and her two brothers and two sisters, had swum in a deep pond of Catholicism as children. Lisa loved God. Jesus. The Eucharist. The Church. Even the Sacrament of Confession.

Getting out of the car to meet Christopher and Emily, she calmed her mind.

"Enough of this death talk already," she thought.

She walked into the lobby. Saw Emily. Smiled. And instantly hugged her.

"What a great night last night!" she delighted. "I'm so lucky. Thanks for meeting me today before you go back to Memphis. I love you so much!"

Lisa smiled as her mind silently wondered, "And why in the world didn't you bring Noah?"

VII. DEEP REFLECTIONS

Emily beamed as she embraced her mother.

"It really was a great night last night, Mom. I hope you were pleased."

"I have no words, Em. No words. It was just the *best*. Wow!" Lisa replied.

Christopher slipped into the booth as his mother and sister were being seated. "Happy sixtieth Mom! You looked so happy last night. I was really, really proud of you."

"Thank you, baby boy. Having all three of you, and all my family and friends together. I couldn't have asked for a better celebration. My heart is so full."

She didn't want it to, but seeing Christopher reminded Lisa of his haunting words at the funeral in her dream. And she couldn't help but wonder as she gazed into his face, "Am I really a good mom? Have I given you all the love I could?"

She quickly regained her composure, and ordered a cup of coffee. No wine today. Not after having had one too many glasses of Chardonnay last night at the birthday fiesta.

Lisa, Emily, and Christopher enjoyed lunch together. Lisa and Emily shared a large Cobb salad while Christopher ordered the Reuben sandwich and fries. Mother and daughter looked on enviously as he ate each french fry. Temptation is often served deep-fried, with salt.

With pleasure, the three savored favorite moments from the party.

"I'll always remember that look on your face, Mom," Christopher said. "When you walked into the Bistro, it was just priceless. You really had no idea, did you?" Christopher inquired.

"Nope. No clue whatsoever, son."

Lisa passed the basket of breadsticks to Emily.

"I've gotta say, I was kinda shocked when Jen mentioned your faith and the Church, Mom. What was that all about? Has she quit church altogether?" Emily asked.

"Not really sure, Em," Lisa answered. "That surprised me too. But it did feel nice to know that she admires me like that. I wouldn't have expected that at all."

Again, Lisa could not keep her heart from looking into the mirror of self-doubt.

"I really hope I've planted enough faith seeds in you two kids and your brother," she thought to herself.

Eventually, Christopher needed to return to work.

Then, Emily's husband, Ron, arrived, eager to head back to Memphis.

Lisa found herself wishing the lunch didn't have to end.

Mother and daughter hugged one last time.

Emily promised to come home again soon. And Lisa declared for all to hear, "I'll be coming to Memphis before you know it!"

She was more than ready to enjoy a weekend with Noah. And to provide Emily and Ron a date night for some precious time by themselves.

"Most of all," Lisa thought, "I want to spend every moment I can holding that little Noah and giving him every ounce of grandmother love in my heart."

VIII. REGRET, PARTY OF ONE?

Lunch with Christopher and Emily proved to Lisa once again what a beautiful treasure her children were.

Yet, for some reason, her mind drifted back to Brian as she drove home alone.

In the past eight years, she thought she had learned not to dwell on his death.

No one prepares you to be a widow at age fifty-two. And it had taken Lisa a while to regain her equilibrium. To feel confident enough about herself and about life to reenter the world. Surrounded by her faithful friends, she had tried mightily to move onward and upward into life—both as a real estate agent and as a new grandmother. Life brought change whether she invited it or not.

Lisa had proven to herself—and evidently to others judging by their remarks at the birthday party—that she was tougher than she had imagined. A ninja? No. But she clearly possessed a persistence and a courage her friends admired.

These recent memories of Brian took Lisa by surprise. She wrote it off as having been triggered by the dream of her own death and her sixtieth birthday.

Some memories generated gratitude. Their college days. The births of their three children. The adventure of moves to places around the country as Brian set out on his career. The camaraderie of taking on life and the world together.

Brian had made her feel safe. She appreciated how he had always earned enough so she never felt crushing financial pressure.

She missed his tender touch. When you're a widow, the days and nights can become cold without the little touches and kind words from your mate. No one to surprise you with an unexpected hug from behind or a casual kiss on the cheek. No one to say, "You look beautiful this morning."

Unlike before Brian's death, Lisa now needed to work. So she had gone from working as a part-time pre-school teacher to becoming a full-time real estate agent. She had made the adjustment.

This percolating brew of memories made Lisa restless. She didn't particularly enjoy remembering

Brian's death and its rocky aftermath. And yet here she was.

One day in particular remained scared in her memory. Five days after Brian had died, the bank called with a question. Lisa had no idea what to do.

Brian had paid the bills for the most part. She knew only a little about their financial life. The funeral Mass had been just two days prior, and now here was the bank on the phone checking to see why a payment had not arrived in its normal fashion.

What happened next still made Lisa as mad as a boiled owl. She searched Brian's computer for logins and passwords. She found nothing—no passwords, no access.

She rummaged through files in his home office for a record of those key accounts and their passwords. Perhaps a list he had maintained in case someone (like his own wife!) needed access in a pinch. Again, nothing.

She asked the kids for help. They took turns sifting through Brian's possessions. No passwords were located but one good thing resulted: They gave away all his clothes to the Salvation Army.

After three days, Lisa still had no sense of her own financial well-being and stability. What funds did she have? Which institutions held them? How could she access them? Where were those dang passwords that seemed like the elusive holy grail?

The process of then building that information from scratch took her more than a year. Waiting on bills and notifications to arrive in the mail just to give her a sense of what her life looked like now, account by account.

She felt like a five-year-old, learning to read by piecing together letters for the first time. It was humiliating.

The fact that Brian had never taken the simple step of letting her know how to locate the basics of their financial life infuriated her. As did the idea that she had never asked him to do so. His thoughtlessness, and their carelessness together, had turned her life topsy-turvy.

She had lived each day in fear, not knowing what bills might arrive. She walked to the mailbox with dread. Keeping Brian's phone activated allowed her to anxiously check his email account. Worst of all was the frustration of having to prove her identity to strangers over and over again to gain access to what rightfully belonged to her.

Fortunately, their attorney had possessed a copy of Brian's will. Without that, Lisa's life would have taken a detour for a decade rather than just a year and a half. But that didn't console her heart much.

Every so often, the traumatic memories of the situation resurfaced. And she found it difficult to forgive Brian.

Driving home this day, Lisa wondered how different her life would have looked had she married someone else. Someone a little more attentive. A man more emotionally invested in his marriage and his family. Someone who really included her in his life.

She had not allowed herself to think or to feel these things before.

She realized her life had reached a turning point. Her fourth quarter was indeed beginning. And she knew one thing for sure: She did not want to enter it pushing a wheelbarrow full of ghosts and regrets.

IX. DON'T BE SILLY

Jen and Amy called with an invitation.

A week had passed since Lisa's birthday bash. It was time to get the gang together again. Time for the Wine (Whine) Girls. Lunch at the Bistro.

Lisa grew excited thinking about seeing Jen and Amy. She was ready to share some of her dream with her best friends.

The ladies gathered around the familiar front-window table. Their little escape bunker away from the cares of the world.

Each ordered a glass of white wine: Lisa her Chardonnay. Jen a Chenin Blanc. And Amy a pour of Riesling, her German favorite.

Jen couldn't stop talking today. She shared news from Kevin's mother. Worries about her daughter's growing reclusiveness. The announcement of a big tennis tournament she really wanted Amy and Lisa to play in. And her anticipation of their beach weekend. Nothing made Jen prattle like planning a trip to the beach.

Amy updated her friends about her son, Craig. He had just received a new promotion and anticipated a new assignment in Asia any day now. He'd had enough of being stationed in Germany.

"So does that mean you're gonna have to switch to sake, Amy?" Jen asked wryly.

Lisa could barely get a word in.

"Jen must have had too much espresso this morning," Lisa thought to herself. "She just won't calm down. She's yapping like an addled chihuahua waiting by the door for its master to take it outside."

Finally, as lunch wound down, Lisa spoke. "You know I've been thinking a lot lately."

"That doesn't sound like you," Jen laughed. "You've been thinking a lot? About what?"

"I dunno. I had this dream about a week ago. My mind just keeps turning it over and over again. Like a roulette wheel that won't stop and the little ball keeps bouncing all over the place."

"Tell us about your dream," Amy kindly suggested. "That sounds intriguing. Jen, try to shut up for five minutes. Lisa hasn't spoken twice all day."

Lisa began to lay out her dream.

The traffic.

The wreck.

The sudden darkness and quiet.

Then the hovering over her own funeral at Sacred Heart parish.

Finally, the sparse, joyless crowd.

Amy listened attentively. She looked directly at Lisa and hung on every word.

Jen, on the other hand, seemed distracted. She kept checking her phone. Like she was waiting on an urgent message from Kevin or maybe her doctor.

Finally, Lisa finished with the haunting words of her own son at the dream funeral. "Do all parents think they are a nine or a ten? Is that a thing? When really they are just a five or maybe a six?"

She fell quiet and let the dream, and Christopher's words, sink in.

Then she asked, "So ... what do y'all think?"

"That's really something," Amy said. "Wow. I bet it's related to Brian's death and your being a widow for these eight years. And you turning sixty and all that. You're bound to start thinking about these kinds of things. Thank you for sharing it with us."

Jen jumped in.

"Yeah, Amy's probably right. It really hit me last year on my sixtieth birthday too. That's a big number, you know? Just means you'd better go ahead and sign up for the tennis tournament. We gotta do this kind of stuff while our bodies still can. We ain't gonna be here forever. And Amy, were you going to look for a house at the beach for our girls' getaway weekend or did you want me to do that? We need to get that locked down sooner rather than later."

Lisa didn't know how to respond. This dream had touched her in a deep place. So she had shared these intimate feelings with her two best friends. And now Jen was changing the subject to tennis and the beach?

"How could she dismiss this so quickly?" she wondered. "And for something as simple as tennis and the beach?

"Do they not see that something is changing in me? More importantly, why does Jen not really even seem to care?"

X. HOPE TO GO

Saturday morning. Lisa leapt from her bed with a rush.

Her Saturdays swelled with a purpose her weekdays just didn't possess.

She volunteered as one of ten Saturday Servants at Sacred Heart each week after the eight a.m. Mass. The pastor would pray a blessing over the group and the parishioners they would be visiting. Then, off the Saturday Servants would go.

Some went to a nearby nursing home, others to a hospice or the community hospital, and Lisa to three women, each living in the home of a family member. She delighted in visiting with each lady before sharing Communion and praying. Good conversation. Good people.

The idea of someone being separated from the parish and the body and blood of Jesus made Lisa's heart hurt. No one deserved to be left out. And this time on Saturdays offered her a chance to play a small role in preventing that.

Plus, she truly enjoyed the conversations.

Charlene, eighty-eight, lived with her daughter. Charlene's mobility had declined over the past few years. Osteoporosis had done its insidious work on her spine. So much so that she really couldn't go anywhere without considerable assistance. Walking even the shortest distance felt like an ascent up Mount Everest to her.

Jo, ninety-one, received care from her son and daughter-in-law. Still mentally as sharp as a razor, Jo loved to talk. She shared memories from her childhood growing up on a farm in the Dakotas: the cold brutal winters, and the warmth their family shared in struggling to survive together.

Nearing one hundred now, Lois surprisingly still lived with her husband in the home they had shared for almost seventy years. The two of them were natives of Tennessee and had grown up in the mountains around Jefferson City. Her husband, Thomas, an engineer, cared for Lois with attentive detail. His love for her miraculously overrode his own physical failings. Each day he managed to bathe her, prepare her meals, and sit with her for hours, holding her hand as she lay in the hospital bed in their living room. Thomas inspired Lisa.

She enjoyed her work, driving clients around Nashville. But Saturdays were special. Listening to these women gave her insight into her own life. And it stirred a sense of gratitude, like she really was a part of something far larger than herself.

XI. ANTHONY

After visiting her homebound friends, Lisa returned to the parish.

She hoped to visit with Fr. Juan for a few minutes. She wanted to share her dream with someone who would listen and offer a helpful perspective. Frankly, she really just wanted to feel heard. And Fr. Juan truly knew how to listen. Unlike Fr. Lawrence, their pastor, whose aloofness defined every interaction.

As she walked in the front door of the church, Lisa bumped into Anthony. Not so much bumped into as ran over, really. She had been so preoccupied with finding Fr. Juan that she wasn't paying attention and nearly toppled the ninety-seven-year-old Anthony.

A widower now for eighteen years, Anthony Martin was revered by the parish as a man who loved generously and loved well. He had cared for his wife, Mary, for nearly a decade as she slowly disappeared into the fog of Alzheimer's disease.

Anthony's career had involved hospital administration. In retirement, then, it only made sense for him to become a Saturday Servant taking Communion to parishioners in the hospital. Even at age ninety-seven, still Anthony persisted in showing up each Saturday.

Short, slim and bald, he wore a Vanderbilt ball cap and rode along with another volunteer to the hospital each week to share the body of Christ there. Always sporting khaki slacks, old tennis shoes, and wire-frame glasses, Anthony faithfully showed up early for eight o'clock Mass. Lisa usually strolled in the door five minutes after Mass had already begun.

Today, however, she practically tackled him in the narthex of the church. She quickly grabbed him to stabilize his small frame.

Steadied, he happily said, "Good morning! How are you today, Lisa?"

She smiled and relaxed. Anthony's infectious grin put people at ease. He usually looked disheveled. But Lisa had never seen him not smiling. Ever.

"I'm so sorry, Anthony," she replied. "I almost wiped you out just then. I guess I just got in too big of a hurry. Please forgive me. Please."

Again, Anthony smiled.

And said nothing.

It occurred to Lisa that he might actually be listening to her. And frankly, she was thirsty just to have someone pay attention to what she had to say.

"You know, I've always wanted to get to know you better, Anthony. I'd really like to learn more about your life. I hear all these good things about you, and it makes me want to know more. And also learn how much of what I've heard is true."

They both chuckled. Anthony blushed.

"Could I buy you a cup of coffee sometime?" Lisa asked. "It would be a privilege to hear about your life. And right now, I've got a few questions about my own. I've been a widow for eight years. Still trying to figure some things out. It'd be great just to chat with someone like you. I think I'd learn a lot."

Anthony nodded. "I'd love to. Can't meet you today, though. Got stuff here to do with some men in the parish. I'd be happy to meet you after we do our thing at the hospital next Saturday morning. Would that work? Saturdays tend to be my best days, when I get out and stir around and all that."

"Next Saturday would be perfect. Thank you, Anthony. That sounds great. How about we meet right here again? I promise not to assault you like I did today. I'm gonna look forward to it all week."

"God bless you. I look forward to a good talk. See you next Saturday. I'll wear a helmet just to be safe," Anthony laughed as he walked away.

Lisa grinned. A new friend. Someone who might truly listen. And someone who had probably accumulated wisdom she could benefit from.

It had been a while since she had actually spoken to someone at the parish. Usually, she had her rhythm, her routine of when she went, who she saw, and where she sat. Today had disrupted that predictability. And she was glad.

She excitedly made a note in her phone not to schedule any clients or friends next Saturday. A new friend had entered her world.

Lisa walked out of the church. It never occurred to her that she had not gotten to see Fr. Juan. Somehow in the tornado of running over Anthony and making coffee plans, her original intention had entirely slipped away.

XII. COFFEE

Lisa's anticipation bubbled up like water from a spring.

She found herself regularly distracted throughout the week as she rehearsed in her mind what she wanted to ask Anthony.

They smiled at each other as she walked into morning Mass at eight o'clock sharp. Once the Saturday Servant team members received Fr. Juan's blessing, Lisa spoke quickly to Anthony.

"I'll see you back here in about two hours. I'm looking forward to our coffee together."

Anthony nodded and smiled.

And the Saturday Servants set off into the community to share faith, hope, and love.

Afterward, the two met in the parking lot. He asked if she would drive him to coffee and then kindly drop him off at his house later. She happily agreed.

They sat at a small table in the Queen Bee, a coffee shop near the parish, and began to talk.

Lisa spoke first. "Anthony, I've heard so much

about you. Tell me a little about your life. I'd love to hear some of your background. I bet your story is fascinating."

"Not really fascinating. But it's true anyway," Anthony laughed. "You probably know my beautiful bride, Mary, passed away almost twenty years ago. Alzheimer's. I quit my job at the hospital and retired when we received her diagnosis. I really wanted to care for her as long as I could. And God was merciful. We were able to care for her at home all the way to the end."

Lisa looked Anthony directly in the eye so he would know she really wanted to hear what he had to say.

"Mary and I had two children. Lucy. My baby girl. We lost her when she was in college. She was driving home from school for a visit. On a mountain road in East Tennessee. Her wheel slipped off the edge of the road. It was awful. She was just nineteen. I don't know that I'll ever get over the horror of receiving that visit from the police."

Anthony paused. His eyes indicated his mind was briefly visiting a faraway place.

"But again, God has been good. I know she's entered the sacred heart of Jesus Himself. That's one reason I love our parish. Sacred Heart. The name itself just means so much to me."

"Oh, I'm so sorry, Anthony," Lisa replied gently. "I had no idea about Lucy. I can't even imagine that kind of pain. I have three children and the thought of losing one is almost unbearable. I'm so very sorry. You've really suffered a lot, Anthony."

He didn't hesitate. "I used to know a priest who said the strangest thing. Fr. James. No matter what kind of news someone shared with him—maybe something good like a child's birth or maybe something painful like a cancer diagnosis—Fr. James always said the same thing. Sometimes, it really shocked people. He'd say, 'That's great! I can't wait to see how God shows you His love through this!'"

Anthony paused and took a sip of coffee.

Lisa let the silent moment just sit.

"In some situations, it seemed like such a jarring thing to say," Anthony continued. "But Fr. James said it with enthusiasm every time because he really meant it. And he's right. Anything I go through is an opportunity for me to experience the love of God in a way I never could in any other way. That love's definitely not just in the good times. It flows in the worst moments of life too. It's non-negotiable. God loves me. More than I can ever know. And you too, by the way.

"We each try to live into that love as fully as we can. A lot of folks don't get that. But I bet you do. Being a widow as young as you are. Taking Communion to people who rarely leave their own home. I imagine you understand."

"I don't know," Lisa shared.

"I'd like to understand that. Would really love to live that way too. But I'm still trying to figure stuff out. You said you had two kids. Tell me some more about that, Anthony."

"Yes, yes indeed," he blurted.

"Our son, Gabriel. He's sixty-two now. I just love him! Teaches chemistry at Middle Tennessee State down in Murfreesboro. He's married. They have four kids. And those four grandchildren have meant it all to me.

"Jacob, he's thirty-eight. He has two children. I get to see him and his family now and then. Christmas and usually a good chunk of the summer they spend near here.

"Teresa, she's thirty-six. Lives in Indy. I'd really like to see her and her three kids more. We FaceTime a lot. Thank God for that technology stuff. They gave me a smartphone years ago and even showed me how to text and get photos from all of them. I'm a ninety-seven-year-old techno-geek!"

Lisa laughed.

"Then there's little Mary, named after my wife," Anthony continued. "She's here in Nashville. Two kids. Come to see me at least once a month. A real treasure. We play cards, watch some TV. They always bring a meal so we can just eat together. I'm so grateful for their thoughtfulness.

"And finally, Billy. He just turned thirty. He's here too. Still single. Not sure if he's staying single on purpose to help me or what. He's good-looking enough. Dark, curly hair. The girls love him. But that's how it's worked out. He comes over all the time. Just hangs out. Never seems to be in a rush. He sells software or something. Sets his own hours. Even spends the night with me every few weeks. And when I'm really lucky, he goes to Mass with me. Doesn't happen a lot, but when it does, I realize the Haitians are right when they say, 'God is sweet.'"

Lisa looked Anthony in the eye. "You are a very blessed man. What a remarkable journey. Mary's Alzheimer's. A long career. The loss of Lucy. Gabriel and his four children and their obvious love for you. And did I count seven great-grandchildren in all that? Wow. I'm impressed. And a little envious too, I've gotta say."

He grinned.

Before she realized it, more than two hours had passed. And Anthony was beginning to look tired.

"Are you ready to head home?" she asked.

"That would be great. Will you please drop me at my house?"

"I'd be happy to. I've enjoyed this so much. What a privilege to hear some of your story. Your journey inspires me so much. Thank you for sharing this with me."

"Thank you, Lisa. It's not often someone really listens. Especially to me. I guess that comes with getting old. So, thank you for listening. I'm grateful."

"Anthony, I'll get you home. And I'd really like to do this again sometime. I've got some questions for you. Stuff I'm trying to figure out in life. I'd love to get your wisdom. Is that OK with you?"

"You want to get wisdom from *me*?" he replied. "That sounds wonderful. Imagine that—a young woman asking an old man for his opinion. Sounds like a great way to spend a day to me."

Lisa smiled at being called a young woman. That certainly had not happened in a long while. Probably about as often as it sounded like someone really listened to Anthony.

Maybe the two of them had more in common than she realized.

XIII. NO REGRETS

The next time Lisa and Anthony met at the Queen Bee, she did most of the talking.

And he displayed the careful listening skills of a good mentor.

Lisa set the table for the conversation. A little about her childhood. The faith of her parents. Her dreams of a life spent as an artist. College. Marriage. Children. Brian's sudden death. The mess he had left behind. Her moments of gratitude. And her moments of regret.

Then she served the meal: Her dream.

Just like she had done with Amy and Jen a couple of weeks prior at lunch, Lisa again sketched out the details of her dream for Anthony. The accident. The darkness. The hovering over her own funeral and observing the joylessness of the small gathering. Finally, the cold, haunting words of Christopher.

"She was OK."

"I think she thought she was more generous than she actually was."

"I loved her, but … "

Lisa spoke these words slowly. Partly for Anthony to really hear them. But mainly because they hung on her heart like an overweight backpack on a long hike.

When she had finished, Anthony said nothing. He simply sat quietly. Absorbing all she had just placed before him. It really had been a full meal of memories, disappointments, hopes, and dreams.

Finally, he simply said, "Thank you, Lisa. These are some deep feelings you're having. And that dream. That's really something. I appreciate your vulnerability in offering that to me. You're special to trust me like that."

A tear slipped out of the corner of Lisa's eye.

"It feels so good to have someone pay attention," she thought to herself.

She opened her heart a bit more and inquired, "Anthony, now, can I ask for your help?"

"Of course," he replied.

"I just turned sixty. My friend's husband, Kevin, says I've entered the fourth quarter of my life. Most women live to be about eighty. Maybe a little more if they're lucky. So I'm three-fourths of the way there.

One quarter to go."

Anthony chuckled. "Mathematically, I guess he's right. You make me laugh. Because now that I'm ninety-seven, I feel like God gave me overtime after the fourth quarter. I got a bonus!"

She gave thanks for this new friend.

"I'd like some of your wisdom," she continued. "I saw how Brian died. So sudden. Unprepared. And now I've had this dream. Received it, really. That's definitely not the funeral I want. I've got all kinds of questions, I guess. But the main one is this: How do I make sure that I finish well?"

"What do you mean?" Anthony asked in return.

"I guess what I'm asking is, how do I make my fourth quarter count? That I live these next twenty years—maybe they're all I get or maybe I get lucky like you and get some overtime—but how do I live them really well?

"It's clear to me. I'm in a different season of my life now. I'm sixty. Men's heads no longer turn when I walk into a room. I'm a widow. I'm kind of invisible, really.

"I have a grandchild with more coming soon. And

I know there's a finish line ahead. I always knew that. But after this dream, I really actually *know* it now.

"In other words, when you know the finish line is real—when you know it's coming sooner than it has occurred to you before—how do you live? That's what I mean: How do I finish my life well?"

Anthony grinned.

She responded, "You sure do grin a lot. I like that! You're ninety-seven, and you seem really happy and content. I like that even more. I think you've learned something I need to discover. So I'm asking: What's the secret?"

"Well, it's funny you should ask me this, Lisa. No one's really ever done that before. I have people come up to me all the time and say, 'When I get old, I hope I'm as happy as you are.' But I've never had anyone ask me how I do it or what I recommend. This is quite an honor.

"And you're right. You'll need wisdom for what you're calling this fourth quarter. In fact, you may need it now more than ever before in your life."

She nodded. "If I hadn't had that dream, I'm not sure I would've asked. But God has gotten my attention. So I'm all ears."

"Well, I've watched a lot of people age. And I've watched a lot of them die. Some have done it really well. And honestly some really have not."

"So, what makes the difference?" Lisa probed. "I'd like to figure out how to do it really well."

"It sounds like you're looking for a way to live, age and die with no regrets."

"That's exactly what I'm looking for. How to age gracefully. And how to die well. Satisfied, really. You're spot-on. I wanna do just that."

Anthony paused before he spoke. "Lisa, first I want you to know that I'm going to start praying for you each day. God has put us together, and I'm really grateful for that. I never had anyone really pray for me until my Mary received her Alzheimer's diagnosis. From that point on, two friends committed to pray for us each day. And it made all the difference. It's powerful. So I want to do that for you.

"Second, I have something I want to give you. It'll help you on this journey you're on. I don't have it with me today, so I'll bring it the next time we get together.

"But right now, it's getting late. I'm tired. And I need to get home."

part three

THE WAY

"For the unlearned, old age is winter; for the learned, it is the season of the harvest."

— Hasidic saying

XIV. THE FIVE KEYS

The following Saturday arrived with a bright sky and a warm breeze. Perfect for sitting outside. Anthony and Lisa found a table on the edge of the Queen Bee's patio. Private enough that no one would overhear their conversation.

Anthony held a small manila envelope in his arthritic right hand.

Lisa's curiosity swelled.

"What *is* that, Anthony?"

Anthony grinned. "Well, Lisa, I'm about to share something with you that I've never shared with anyone."

"Really?!" She felt honored.

"Yep. I've debated this in my mind for several days. But you're the only person who's ever asked me why I seem so happy at the ripe old age of ninety-seven. So I'm about to offer you my recipe, with all my secret ingredients."

Lisa anticipated his words as if she had scaled a

grand mountain to receive wisdom from a hermit living at the top.

"In this envelope are lots and lots of notes," Anthony began. "Notes jotted and scribbled over the years. Notes taken here and there while I've watched good friends, as well as complete strangers—all kinds of people in their 'golden years.' I've watched them live. Some struggle; some thrive.

"And I've watched many people die. I've even watched my sweet Mary die. Way too soon. Mary and I talked about aging and dying a lot as she slipped away."

Anthony paused.

Lisa looked deeply into his kind eyes and waited silently until he spoke again.

"There are some very real advantages to living to be ninety-seven. You get to see a lot. If you really pay attention, you can learn a lot. I've tried to do that. I wanted to know what you want to know now: How can I finish my life well? And I've discovered the five keys to living and dying with no regrets."

He extracted a single piece of paper from the envelope.

"These five insights have formed the foundation for me. But before I share this with you, I want you to know one thing: It's gonna be OK, Lisa. It really is. Just because you're aging doesn't mean there's not a place for you anymore. You really can have a marvelous fourth quarter."

Anthony then handed Lisa the paper.

The 5 Keys to Living and Dying with No Regrets

Say Yes to God
God invites you onto a wonderful journey.
When you say yes to God's invitation, you know
where you're going.

Focus on a Fourth Quarter Virtue
Pursue one fourth quarter virtue God has specifically
placed in you. Then watch it create blossoms in all
areas of your life.

Give. It. Away.
The more you give yourself away,
the happier you'll be.

Forgive. Often.
Bitter and resentful is no way to live.
And it's definitely no way to die.

Be Open to Life
Your fourth quarter can be more of a birthing than a
dying. Be open to what can be.

XV. SAY YES TO GOD

Anthony looked at his notes. Then took a sip of coffee.

He hoped his words would calm Lisa's anxiety about the future and help her to pursue it wholeheartedly.

"I'm going out of town for a couple of weeks," he told her. "Maybe even a whole month. Not really sure to be honest.

"My granddaughter, Teresa, is picking me up tomorrow and taking me to be with her family in Indy. I can't wait! I've been hoping for this for a long time— just to be with them with no schedule and no rush. Carefree timelessness with the people I love so much.

"Not sure I'll ever get to do this kind of thing again, so I'm gonna make the most of it. You won't be able to reach me for a while.

"For right now, I want to share a few thoughts about what I've just given you. Then, you take a little time to reflect on it while I'm gone. See what you think. And when I get back, let's get together again. I'd love to hear how it's going for you. OK?"

Lisa nodded, eager to hear more.

Anthony resumed.

"First, say yes to God. This almost seems obvious, doesn't it? But it's important for me to start with this.

"It's first for a reason. Because people with a robust faith life live and die very differently than those who do not. I've just seen it so many times. You can't fake it.

"As you age, God invites you onto a wonderful journey with Him.

"You're either on that journey to God and with God, or you're not.

"Some folks try to play pretend. It's like they're putting up pretty wallpaper, but there's no wall there. Just a board or two. It's flimsy. Like wallpaper just flapping in the wind.

"But when someone really spends time with the Lord. Gives themselves over to His heart. It shows. It's beautiful. And it's real. Makes all the difference in your fourth quarter. Because you know who you are. And you know where you're going.

"You know what matters most. And you also know what matters least.

"Without that faith life, folks are just lost. Flailing

around trying to cling to people and stuff and memories from earlier in life.

"So my advice for you: Dig the well before you get thirsty. Start now.

"Wherever you are on this journey—and by my observations you're doing great—dig that well. Spend time with Him. Deepen your roots in prayer. Embrace the classroom of silence. Serve Him. Love Him.

"And you'll be just fine."

XVI. FOCUS ON A FOURTH QUARTER VIRTUE

"Now the second key: Focus on a fourth quarter virtue. I could talk about this one for hours."

Anthony stopped and nodded at the waitress as she offered a warm-up refill for his cup.

"It's so powerful. And it took me a long time to figure this out: Identify the virtue you believe God has placed in you specifically for your fourth quarter. Choose it. Claim it. Own it. You'll know the one for you when you listen.

"Then, pick a habit to fertilize it. Pursue that virtue. And watch it grow.

"Focus on pursuing that one fourth quarter virtue, and it will create blossoms in all the other areas of your life. Just like the roses in your garden you've told me so much about.

"Take my friend, Arthur. He goes to Sacred Heart too. Maybe you know him.

"A real leader. President of a think tank. Wrote oodles of books and articles about important topics in his field. Consulted by world leaders.

"When he entered his late fifties, he realized he didn't have the drive or the creativity his younger colleagues possessed. His mental processing speed, and his ability to analyze things, no longer met his own high standard.

"But Arthur also realized he had accumulated enormous wisdom over his decades of experience. He had always wanted to coach and prioritize people. The demands of his life just had prevented him from doing it.

"So he transitioned. From being the primary executive leader in his organization. To becoming more of a trusted sage. Younger members took over the reins to lead. And Arthur moved on to sharing his wisdom with the team rather than directing it.

"He became a master teacher. He shared his experience with others. He walked alongside younger talent and helped it emerge. No more overwhelming responsibilities of that executive role. Arthur discovered a new purpose.

"He's past seventy now. Springs out of bed in the morning. Satisfaction with life leaps off his face. He's done just what this second secret says. He's built his fourth quarter around the virtue of wisdom. Pursuing it. Growing it. Sharing it.

"In my life, God has focused me on the virtue of patience. He began to grow that virtue in me as my wife slipped into the arms of Alzheimer's. Perhaps that patience had been in me all my life, but I never knew it. I'll tell you more about that when we get together again.

"Here's my point: Embrace that virtue God is urging in you. Pay attention to it.

"God has planted a talent or a gift in you. It's there ready for you to discover, or even recover, for this fresh season in your life. Like it's been sitting there inside you, dormant, just waiting to sprout and create new life.

"And what He has planted in you may be very different from the talents and gifts you've used in earlier portions of your life.

"Who knows what your fourth quarter virtue might be?

"Just know it can really fuel your life now. That's all I'm saying."

XVII. GIVE. IT. AWAY.

Lisa feverishly took notes on the legal pad she had brought. Trying to drink in all the wisdom Anthony was pouring out from his fount.

"Look at the third key," he began.

"Give. It. Away.

"Give your knowledge away.

"Give your experience away.

"Give your money away.

"Give your stuff away.

"Give your love away.

"Give your life away.

"Give it all.

"Away.

"The more you give yourself away, the happier you'll be.

"The world will teach you just the opposite. But don't be deceived. The more you give away your life, the more life you will have.

"We spend the first chunk of life acquiring stuff: reputations, degrees, status, possessions. All of that.

"But the happiest people I know spend the fourth quarter giving it all away.

"It's just so transformational.

"The human heart is made to give. But sometimes our hearts are stopped up—constipated, sluggish, unwilling.

"Your heart wasn't made to cling to love. It's made to share it.

"The more you give, the healthier your heart will be."

XVIII. FORGIVE. OFTEN.

"Next comes a crucial piece of wisdom," Anthony continued.

"Number four. Forgive. Often.

"I'm giving it to you straight up: Bitter and resentful is no way to live. And it's definitely no way to die.

"I see this over and over again. People who get all tangled up in old wounds and sticky resentments. They wander around in that labyrinth of lingering hurts and never find their way out. Lost in the past. Can't step into what life is or might be.

"In fact, I witnessed it again just the other day. A mother and father estranged from one of their three children for oh so many years. The father died last week. So the family's oldest child, Heather, reached out to the youngest son, the estranged one. That son told his own sister (by email because he wouldn't even take a phone call—that's how bad it was), 'Heather, please don't call me. Just send me a note when Mom and Dad are both dead.'

"Think of all the wasted time in that tortured, painful relationship—all the time keeping score, nurturing the resentment. It's like trying to use poison to fertilize your garden. That negativity just eats you up from the inside out. It kills you. And it's also killing the people around you all along the way.

"Forgive.

"Let. It. Go.

"When you're facing death, you realize just how little any of that junk matters. I wasted so much time earlier in my life holding grudges and being angry for no good reason. I wish I'd have just let it all go and chosen to be happy instead.

"And please don't forget to forgive yourself. Otherwise, you'll imprison yourself in shame. Guilt you can work with. Guilt can help you grow. But shame infects and destroys your soul.

"Enough of that. The solution is simple.

"Forgive often.

"Forgive completely.

"Forgive well.

"Period."

XIX. BE OPEN TO LIFE

"Finally, the fifth key to living and dying with no regrets," Anthony declared.

"Let me share some thoughts about that and then we're done for today. I've given you plenty to noodle on while I am away these next few weeks.

"Be open to life. That's the final one.

"Be open. Kind of says it all, doesn't it?

"It might even be the gateway to all of this.

"Be open.

"Your fourth quarter isn't just some extension of your third quarter. It's not just more and better of what you've already been doing or what you already have in your life.

"Things change.

"Embrace that change. And you'll discover this new season can be more of a birthing than a dying.

"Resist the urge to shut down, close off, or just play it safe. I watch people do that all the time. They're scared of aging. They get guarded and cautious. Their world gets smaller and smaller by the day.

"Do the exact opposite.

"Explore new things. Seek new possibilities. Add new friends.

"Don't simply settle for the easy or the comfortable. Don't cling to what was. You'll grow stale and brittle.

"Be open to what can be."

Anthony stopped. He took a deep breath and grinned at Lisa.

She paused her writing and placed her yellow legal pad on the table. "Thank you, Anthony. This is just so rich. My mind is racing. And my heart is full. Thank you."

"Thank *you*," he said. "It's been good for me to share these five secrets. I never would've done it if you hadn't asked. Like I said, take a little time to reflect on all this. And let's have coffee again when I get back."

Lisa hugged Anthony as they got up to leave. "I sure do love you. What a gift you've given me! I hope you have a wonderful visit with your family."

"Remember, Lisa," he whispered, "I'm praying for

you each day. I can't wait to see what God's going to do in your life."

XX. ABSORBING

When Lisa got home, she put on her bathrobe and curled up on the couch. She pulled an afghan over herself and placed her reading glasses on the bridge of her nose.

Then she studied every word of Anthony's wisdom.

She pored over her notes on the legal pad. Underlining this. Highlighting that. Trying to organize his insights in her mind.

Her focus lingered on a single line:

Your fourth quarter can be more of a birthing than a dying.

"My fourth quarter isn't just more and better of what I've already been doing or what I already have in my life," she thought as she heard Anthony's words once again.

"Things change. And I need to embrace that change. This is a new season."

Her eyes then shifted to the second key:

Pursue one fourth quarter virtue God has specifically

placed in you. Then watch it create blossoms in all areas of your life.

"That's so cool. I wonder what my fourth quarter virtue might be?" Lisa's mind simmered like a Crock Pot with Anthony's insights slowly cooking inside.

She asked God to produce a delicious meal from it.

XXI. THE NAYSAYER

When Lisa prayed, she offered her thoughts and dreams to God. When she drove clients to new neighborhoods, she mulled over Anthony's five keys. When she went to sleep, she found herself turning those ideas over in the tumbler in her head.

Finally, she could no longer keep the conversation to herself. So she invited Jen to grab breakfast.

They met at Eggs n' Grits, Lisa's favorite. She loved grits, and nobody made them better. Even though she had grown up in Illinois, she had acquired a taste for grits as soon as she and Brian had moved to Nashville. Grits with salt and butter. Definitely not sugar. She could eat a breakfast consisting of nothing but that. With a cup of coffee too, of course.

As she and Jen ate, Lisa shifted the conversation from the small talk of kids, weather, and what they had on their schedules for the day to what she really wanted to talk about.

"Jen, you know how I told you I've been doing a lot of thinking lately?"

"Yeah, sure. I remember that. You still doing that thinking? Really seemed to be weighing on you a lot."

"Well, yes, actually. I even had coffee a few times with Anthony, the elderly gentleman at church. Always wears the Vanderbilt ball cap and khakis. You know him?"

"I know who he is. Never met him. I haven't seen him in a while. Thought he might have died. Why did you meet with him?"

"Remember the dream I shared with you and Amy?" Lisa asked.

"A little bit. You still thinking about that?"

"Yeah. It really struck a chord inside me. And the notes keep ringing. I see that funeral. My funeral. The small group of joyless people. Their blank faces.

"And I hear Christopher's words over and over again. About how I was just OK as a parent and not as generous or as loving as I thought I was. Kind of makes you think, doesn't it?"

Jen spoke up. "Lisa, it was just a dream. You turned sixty. You've got a lot of good times ahead of you. Quit thinking about dying all the time. Get over it. Seriously. Take it from a friend. Lighten up and enjoy life, while you still can. Life is short."

Lisa paused and took a deep breath. Then she decided to plow ahead. "When I talked to Anthony, I asked him what he had learned from living to ninety-seven. From caring for his wife who died from Alzheimer's. I asked him how he seemed to be so happy, and so content, every time I saw him."

"OK," Jen replied. "So what did he say?"

"He's actually taken notes over the years. Just watching people in the fourth quarter, like your Kevin said to me. Watching how they live and how they die. But here's what's really cool. He has these five keys to living and dying with no regrets. They're fascinating."

"Watching how people die? That seems a bit morbid."

"Anthony's not weird, Jen. Actually, he's really thoughtful. And intelligent. And unbelievably kind. He listens like nobody I've ever been around before."

"OK. OK. So what did he say he's learned?" Jen asked.

Lisa did her best to share Anthony's wisdom, but she could tell Jen wasn't paying attention. She interrupted Lisa, asked the waitress for more coffee, checked her phone three times, and finally took out her wallet to pay for her part of the breakfast. All while Lisa was trying to share the insights Anthony had offered.

Finally, Lisa asked Jen, "Does this not interest you? Am I boring you? You seem incredibly distracted."

"Honestly, I've got other stuff in my life besides thinking about dying. Stuff like ... not dying. Know what I mean?"

"I get that. But do you ever think about what it means to age gracefully and to die well? To end your life satisfied? Ever?"

"I think about it all the time," Jen pushed back. "That's why I play tennis. Stay fit. Tan. Healthy. I'm trying to make the most of this life and make my body last as long as it can. Every day ... speaking of which, how about doing me a favor? Sign up for this tennis tournament with me. It'll do you some good. And it'll also get your mind off of dying."

Lisa felt perplexed. Why was Jen struggling so much lately even to engage with her?

So she simply smiled and politely replied, "I'll get the check today. I just sold a house and I'm the one who invited you for breakfast. Go play tennis. Enjoy yourself. We'll catch up soon."

XXII. FR. JUAN

A week passed. Lisa's mind continued to percolate with new thoughts.

So she made an appointment with Fr. Juan. She really wanted to have someone listen. And then, offer some wise counsel.

Lisa took a seat in Fr. Juan's office, hoping to share this idea of the fourth quarter.

"I'm not really sure what to do next," she began. "At the same time, I don't feel in too big of a rush, Fr. Juan. I'm just trying to process some ideas. And I'm learning so much. You've always been there for me. And your homilies inspire me. So, can I share with you one thought and get your advice?"

"Certainly," Fr. Juan responded. "I feel honored that you would come see me and ask my opinion."

Lisa shared Anthony's insight about embracing a fourth quarter virtue. Something that fuels and inspires you in this new season of life.

Then she asked, "Does that make sense to you? I was thinking about Arthur. My friend, Anthony

Martin, told me about him. He goes to this parish too. It sounds like he's been driven by the virtue of wisdom all through his sixties and now into his seventies."

"I haven't really thought about it like this before, Lisa," Fr. Juan said. "But you're right. It makes me think about a funeral I did not too long ago.

"Her name was Agnes. Talk about a lady who was close to her destiny. She discovered a whole new sense of mission in her life. And fortitude. I just love that word: Fortitude. Real courage in facing difficulty or danger. That was Agnes.

"She worked in the hospital for years. Then became something like a missionary when she retired. Dedicated her life to serving the poor. Went to some really challenging places in Africa to share the heart of Jesus with children. She invested chunks of time each year in difficult situations. All the way into her eighties.

"She actually died in Cameroon. The brakes in her van failed. The vehicle slipped over the edge of a cliff. It was like she flew straight into eternity.

"Some folks thought that was a tragedy. But I got a letter from her. Received it in the mail about a week after she died. Postmarked from Cameroon. Telling me she was happier than she had ever been. Just beautiful!

"What you're making me realize is that Agnes discovered a new gift for faith and fortitude she never knew she had. When she combined that virtue of fortitude with the compassion she had shown as a nurse, her daring love for God became the most beautiful part of her entire life. I can tell you for certain—she lived and died with no regrets."

Fr. Juan paused.

Then he asked, "So, what do you think your fourth quarter virtue might be?"

She laughed.

"I have no idea. But I'm beginning to think I really want to find out."

XXIII. MORE COFFEE

A week later, Lisa invited Amy to connect.

Jen and Amy had been her trusted friends for decades. And Lisa really wanted to include them in these strange new exhilarating feelings appearing in her soul. She hoped Amy wouldn't bring to the conversation the same discomfort Jen seemed unable to hide.

Lisa shared her thoughts. She showed Amy the sheet of paper Anthony had given her.

Amy listened attentively. She looked into Lisa's eyes. Nodded her head. Even asked a few questions.

As their time came to a close, Lisa asked Amy, "So ... whatcha think?"

"What do I think about what?" Amy answered.

"About all these images and ideas bouncing around in my head like a pinball. All these feelings emerging inside of me. What Anthony had to say. Any of it. Am I crazy?"

A kind smile spread across Amy's face. "I'm the last one to ask about what some of these things mean. Honestly, I just have never really thought about my own death. Maybe I should, I dunno. But I do care about you. And if this is important to you, I care. Can I ask you one question?"

"Sure," Lisa replied.

"You said he mentioned that people with a robust faith life live and die very differently than those who do not."

"Right."

"What does he mean? What in the world is a robust faith life?"

"I'm not really sure either, Amy. But I think he's saying a full faith makes you fully alive. Embracing God. Trusting Him. Really belonging to Him. Not just giving Him an occasional glance or panic prayer like we usually do."

"Hmmmm," Amy sighed.

"What are you thinking about?" Lisa asked gently.

"That forgiveness thing. 'Forgive. Often.' How bitter and resentful is no way to live. And it's definitely no way to die. It's just so true, you know?"

"Yep."

"I'm thinking of two sisters I know," Amy continued. "Both in their eighties. They haven't spoken to each other in decades. Neither one can even remember what they're upset about. Or why they quit talking. They just don't. It's like they're in prison and can't remember why."

"You are so right," Lisa replied.

"Forgive often. Forgive completely. Forgive well. It's just so, so, so true."

The two sat in silence for a minute or two.

"Thank you for letting me open up about this," Lisa said softly. "The whole topic seems to annoy Jen."

"Well, I'm happy to listen. Not sure I can offer you much help, though. Maybe this is just a phase. Hopefully a good one. That dream really did spark something inside you, didn't it? How about this: I promise to pray for you. And when I can help, you feel free to call me. OK?"

Lisa realized Amy cared. She might not understand, but she did care.

And Lisa gave thanks for that.

XXIV. FIRST STEPS

The next evening, after a full day of working with clients, Lisa sat down at the small desk in her bedroom and took out a yellow legal pad.

Maybe it was the artist in her, or maybe it was just her age, but she always liked to start with a pencil and a big piece of blank paper when she was working on something creative. Computers and all that had their place. But that wasn't the starting place for her creativity.

That blank piece of paper returned her to childhood. A little girl making drawings around the house and outside in the yard.

Lisa began to jot down the hurricane of ideas and thoughts swirling in her mind. Hoping to make sense of what God might be up to in her life and what to do next.

Reflecting on Anthony's five keys.

Asking God to inspire her.

Considering what could be.

She dreamed deeply about her own life and how she might live with no regrets.

She wrote it all down, not wanting to judge possibilities or dismiss them too soon. She put every rumination on the paper. Even things that didn't seem like ruminations at all—like "Stop by the grocery tomorrow and get some eggs. Bake a cake."

By the time the clock struck ten that evening, Lisa's yellow pad looked like a spider web of scribblings. Her thoughts, emotions, hopes, and dreams all emerged on the paper. Little prayers. Gifts she knew she had. Talents she wished she had. Gifts she had never used. What gave her passion. What did not. Who she loved. What mattered least. And what seemed to matter most of all.

There's no master class to teach you how to live well, age gracefully, and die peacefully. But Lisa's first steps felt better than good. They felt more like a cleansing—liberating and exciting.

Lisa wasn't sure what her next step would be in trying to map her life for her fourth quarter. But she was open. And by the end of the evening, she knew three things for sure:

1. She had always possessed a love and a talent for art but had rarely used it. Her heart hoped maybe God was up to something with that.

2. She needed to share her faith more intentionally with her growing family. And she knew just the place to start: with an open invitation to join her on Saturday mornings in taking Communion to homebound parishioners. Her family could enjoy this special spiritual time together with her as often as they liked.

3. Dreaming about this new phase of her life could be fun! Anthony's wisdom had real power.

XXV. PUSHBACK

Lisa pushed herself out of bed early and made a cup of coffee.

She said a prayer of thanks for the upcoming day.

Then sat down at her computer to clean out her emails before meeting her first client, a couple moving to Nashville from New Jersey.

The first email to pop up was from Jen. Following up on the tennis tournament invitation:

"Hey Lisa, really need you to go ahead and sign up. Just one slot left. And I want you to be my partner. Hit the link here and sign up today. OK? Thanks, Jen."

Lisa hit Reply:

"Jen, I've been thinking. I'm just not all that into tennis right now. So I think I'm gonna take a pass on this tournament. Thanks for thinking of me. I'll see you soon. Love, Lisa."

She hit Send.

Then spent a few minutes deleting all the spam emails that seemed to grow in her inbox each night like mold reappearing in the shower every day. Then she responded to an email from one of her fellow agents asking about a house.

Before she could close her inbox, another email from Jen arrived:

"Really? Lisa, come on! You're thinking way too much. Seriously. Relax. Enjoy your life. Why are you turning into such an old biddy? Sign up for the stupid tournament already."

Lisa grimaced. Shook her head once. Turned off her laptop and slipped it into her oversized bag.

She got in her car. Started the engine. And began her day of showing houses.

XXVI. EXPLORATION

On Sunday, after Mass, Lisa landed right where she wanted to be: Home alone.

With an entire afternoon and evening free to do as she pleased. No clients. No responsibilities. A rare treat.

She turned on some music. The soothing sounds of Sinatra floated through the room like the trill of birds on a spring morning.

Lisa plopped on her couch and soaked in the fullness of the moment.

And then she asked herself a question: "What do I really want to do with this free time?"

The question danced around her mind for a few minutes. And it gave her pleasure.

The laptop lay before her. Lisa opened it, clicked on her browser, and searched the internet for: "kids and art."

She scanned the results.

Then she searched: "children and art."

Then: "art for kids."

Then: "art kids Nashville."

Her eyes skimmed over all the possibilities: books, art lessons, an art school, even a children's school for the arts.

Her gaze landed on a place she had never encountered in all her years of living in Nashville. "Playful Possibilities: A Place for Children and Art."

Lisa clicked on their website. She poked around the handful of sections there.

About Us.

Donate.

Children and Art.

Nashville Children in Need.

"What an intriguing place," she thought. "How have I never even heard of these people before?"

Playful Possibilities provided a place for local artists to work their craft: studios, displays, that kind of thing.

But most of all, it emphasized providing pathways for children to come watch artists at work—to discover pottery, painting, ceramics, even sculpture.

It encouraged artists to offer classes and coaching for the children. To help them learn the craft for themselves. All for free.

The goal? To help children in need imagine their own contributions and expressions in art. To pass on the beauty of art to children. To focus on children from neighborhoods of great need in Nashville.

Playful Possibilities' motto leapt off the web page and squarely into Lisa's mind: "Inspire. Imagine. Instruct."

Her childhood dreams of becoming an artist peeked around the corner of her soul and smiled.

"Might there be a way to rediscover something I thought I had long since discarded?" she wondered. "And then to share it with children? Especially with children who might otherwise not have the opportunity to explore art and discover their own gifts?"

She dreamed about the role art might regain in her life.

Lisa made a note in her phone to swing by Playful Possibilities sometime when she was showing homes in that area of Nashville.

When she glanced at her watch, it was eleven p.m., well past her bedtime. Somehow, the free afternoon and evening had taken her down a rabbit hole as if she were Alice in Wonderland.

And the adventure had delighted Lisa in a way she never would have expected.

XXVII. CHANGES

Three days later, the delightful fairy dust of anticipation sprinkled Lisa's morning.

First, she showed a client the Franklin area, south of Nashville. She guided the couple through three homes, then took them to lunch.

Afterward, she grabbed a quick cup of coffee and headed downtown. Her afternoon stood open and free on her calendar. She immediately knew how she planned to use it: Playful Possibilities.

Lisa's imagination had been building castles in her mind ever since she had spent that afternoon (and evening) digging around their website. Learning about a mission helping children in need to discover art generated an energy in her like nothing she had experienced since the birth of Noah.

She sipped her coffee and listened to her music.

As she drove, her phone rang. She glanced at the screen on her dashboard; it was Jen calling. She quickly hit the Answer button on her steering wheel and said, "Hey, Jen! What're you doing on this very fine afternoon?"

"Great to hear your voice, girlfriend," Jen replied. "Did you just make a sale or something? You sound so pumped up!"

"Not sure about the sale. Just showed a nice young couple some homes in Franklin. Now I'm on my way to do something I've really been looking forward to. What're you doing?"

"Had some free time. Thought it would be great to catch up. You got time for a cup of coffee? The Queen Bee, maybe?" Jen asked.

"I could meet this evening if you're free. But I can't do it right now. Got something on my mind and I really need to go check it out."

"Please tell me this is not more of your 'thinking a lot lately' thing."

Lisa sighed. "Well, maybe it is. I found some stuff related to what I was trying to tell you and Amy about. An art place for disadvantaged kids in downtown Nashville. I'm gonna spend the afternoon checking that out if they'll let me. It sounds really interesting."

"Come on, Lisa," Jen volleyed. "You can do that anytime. I really want to have a cup of coffee with you. Seriously. I'll meet you at a place near the interstate so you don't have to go too far out of your way."

Lisa's stomach tightened. "Jen, I'd love to see you. Just not right now. Tonight—a glass of wine at the Bistro, maybe? Or tomorrow's pretty free for me too. We could grab some coffee then."

"Never mind. You're lost in this new black hole of 'thinking'," Jen shot back. "It's like I don't even know who you are anymore. You've changed. Never mind. I'll call you later. Bye."

Jen hung up.

Lisa's car fell silent for a moment before the music kicked back in on the speakers. The singer's voice created a new conversation where Jen's had ended.

She continued driving toward Playful Possibilities. Her mind toggled back and forth between delight at this afternoon's upcoming exploration and the sting of her friend's words: "You've changed."

Then again, Lisa realized, maybe she really had changed. She just wasn't sure how.

XXVIII. ENCOURAGEMENT

Lisa invested a full afternoon at Playful Possibilities.

She stared at the sign above the entrance, studying it:

Art is a spiritual pursuit
It is wrestling with the angels
It is dancing with the gods

She slowly walked around the facility and absorbed every activity she encountered.

She visited with some artists.

She listened to the classical music gently wafting throughout the spaces.

She sat in on a classroom of children learning the first steps of a potter's wheel.

She stood beside a sculptor and admired his careful work.

Most of all, Lisa dreamed about the carefree pleasure of sketching scenes in her backyard. She missed art and was delighted to welcome it back into her life.

But she couldn't quite shake off the bite of Jen's brush-off.

Lisa knew what to do: call Amy and get her perspective. If nothing else, at least she would listen.

Amy answered the phone in her gentle voice. "How're you doing, Lisa?"

Lisa shared the highlights of her day and a quick word about her clients. Then she excitedly recounted her visit to Playful Possibilities and the vibrancy she saw there.

"That sounds wonderful. I'm so happy for you. Good for you!" Amy responded encouragingly.

Lisa thanked her and then pivoted. "Jen called right in the middle of it all. Wanted me to drop what I was doing and meet her for coffee. Like we always do. But I had my heart set on visiting Playful Possibilities. Been looking forward to it all week long.

"When I told Jen that, she went all nuclear meltdown on me. Told me I had changed. That she didn't even know who I was anymore. Then she hung up. To be honest, that kind of rattled me. I mean, you and she have been huge friends to me forever. I mean, forever. I love her.

"Is it wrong to wanna do something else and say, 'How about coffee or wine later?'"

Amy listened intently before she responded. "No. You're not crazy. But you do have to admit that your life has been shifting in some new ways lately. Jen just doesn't understand that.

"Frankly, I really don't understand it all either. But I do love you. You can do new things. And that's OK. You don't have to explain everything to me, or to Jen."

"Thank you," Lisa replied. "I'm really just trying to take that dream seriously. I mean, it was so real. And you and I both know God sometimes speaks through dreams.

"Plus, it's true. I *am* going to die. I *will* have a funeral. I *will* be remembered. And I want to make my life count now.

"I don't know what that looks like, really. But I do know I have an energy inside me I haven't had for a long, long time. And to be honest, Playful Possibilities was fun. I like fun. I like joy. Is that so wrong?

"Anyway," she continued, "I know it's late. I'm so grateful for you. Thanks for listening to me. Just wanted to be sure I wasn't losing it."

"I love you, Lisa," Amy softly spoke into the phone. "You're my friend. Nothing can change that. It'll be OK. It really will."

XXIX. RETREAT

At Mass on Sunday, Lisa scampered in the side door at 11:04, and quickly found a seat as the choir was singing the Gloria.

Fr. Lawrence tended to ramble and stray far afoot in his homilies. And today proved to be no exception. Lisa silently wished Fr. Juan were the celebrant today. "Life sure is messy," she thought.

She began to look at the parish bulletin. An announcement of sign-ups for youth ministry. A Knights of Columbus banquet. A message about giving.

Her eyes landed on an image of Mary with the headline "Retreat." She skimmed the words:

What's God Saying to You?
You're Invited
Two Days of Silence
Listening TO God and FOR God
Saturday and Sunday   October 7–8
With Sr. Anastasia, Retreat Leader

at
Our Lady of Mount Carmel Monastery

Lisa had never attended a silent retreat. In fact, she had never wanted to. It sounded so somber and dry. Nuns, monastery, silence. Probably bad food too. Yikes.

But that opening line caught her attention as Fr. Lawrence's homily paraded on.

What's God Saying to You?

Lisa did know for sure she wanted some answers to that question.

So she folded the bulletin and stuck it in her purse to look at again later.

XXX. GETAWAY

When the Wine Girls gathered again at their front table at the Bistro, Amy ushered in their favorite topic: their annual beach getaway weekend.

Just the three of them. No men. No kids. No responsibilities. Pure peace.

Lisa couldn't even remember the first year she and her two best friends had found their way down to the Florida Panhandle to decompress together for a few days. It really had been that long. At least twenty years. Or was it twenty-five?

Amy lit an imaginary "first candle of preparation" for this sacred three-day weekend when she exclaimed, "I've got it! I reserved that condo we loved so much two years ago but was booked last year. You remember? The one that had that pool where we could look out at the Gulf and the sunset in the evening?"

"Perfect!" Jen enthused. "I just loved that place. Great job, Amy. You're the rock star of reservations!"

Amy announced, "I loved it so much that I went

ahead and reserved the whole week. I'm gonna stay an extra day or three depending on how busy Daniel is with work. Unless he really needs me back to help with some project or the bookkeeping. We've got an empty nest now. And I'm not getting any younger. I just want to sit in the peace of that place."

Lisa sighed, longing for the peace of the beach. "That sounds wonderful. The world feels like it's closing in on me lately too."

Jen raised her glass. "Here's to October. To our beach weekend. And to Amy, the gatherer of great women!"

The Wine Girls happily drank to the toast.

Amy smiled broadly. "Mark it down now, ladies. October sixth to eighth. It's gonna be awesome!"

"It's the most wonderful time of the year!" Jen replied.

Lisa quickly scribbled a note on her napkin with the dates to input them on her personal and work calendars later.

She delighted in the idea of some time with friends, away from her routine. "Let the wine and the whining begin!"

The three friends laughed together and dived into their shared appetizer of fried calamari.

With visions dancing in their heads of the fresh Gulf oysters soon to come in October.

XXXI. SIGN-UPS

At Mass that Sunday, Lisa stopped by a table in the narthex and picked up a flyer about the upcoming silent retreat at the Carmelite monastery.

That afternoon, she pondered the wonderful possibilities two days of sheer silence might stir in her. She had never tried anything like that before. A silent retreat. With nuns. It sounded so mysterious.

Lisa glanced at the flyer and its description of the two days. Large blocks of time for prayer. Walking the monastery grounds. Three talks by Sister Anastasia scattered throughout the two days. Mass with a Carmelite priest. Each retreatant assigned a small personal room, or cell. Meals together in silence in the refectory. Attendance strictly limited to the first twelve people to register. All bathed in glorious, uninterrupted silence in a sacred place.

Before long, Lisa had convinced herself to do it.

She toyed with all the questions scampering around in her head.

"What was that much silence really like?

"Could she actually be quiet for that long?

"What would the attendees actually be doing?

"What would they eat?

"Who else might be participating in this retreat?

"What was Sister Anastasia like?"

And then, the most beautiful question of all occurred to Lisa.

"What might God say to me?"

She worried she might hear nothing at all. But she quickly resolved to offer herself completely to God for the two days just to see what would happen.

She pulled out her laptop and went to the website listed on the flyer. Smiling, she signed up.

She had lots of questions. But one thing Lisa knew for sure:

Something wonderful was about to happen in her life.

XXXII. CONFLICT

Lisa always mapped her upcoming week first thing on Monday morning.

Reviewing the clients she expected to meet.

Surveying the homes available in best-selling areas.

Sketching out her days. Whom she would see. Times she would plan to show houses.

And any other appointments that needed to be accommodated.

Today, as she managed her calendar, Lisa thought of the silent retreat. She proudly blocked out those two days, which were now only a few weeks away. October 7–8.

Marking her calendar triggered her memory of the napkin in her purse from the Bistro. The one where she had jotted down the dates for the beach weekend.

She rummaged through her belongings until she found it. She looked at the dates: October 6–8.

The conflict screamed at her like an angry toddler. The silent retreat. And the beloved beach getaway with Jen and Amy. At the same time.

Yikes!

Lisa remembered the great peace that had settled over her last night while she imagined the possibilities for the silent retreat. And the joy she felt when she had registered. The anticipation. The longing to be alone with God. And just listen.

These were not feelings Lisa had encountered often in her life. And she welcomed them.

Quickly she realized what she was going to do. And it surprised her.

After mapping out her week's plan and setting a few other appointments on her calendar for the month ahead, Lisa opened her email.

She began to type:

Ladies, I am soooooo sorry. It's hard for me to believe, but I will not be able to go on the Beach Weekend this year!!!!

I have a conflict. A retreat I signed up for at the parish.

I'm really REALLY sorry. But I'm so excited for you two. I love you both and can't wait to hear all about it. And can't wait to go with you again next year.

Much Love,
Wine Girl Lisa

She then hit Send.

XXXIII. MORE CONFLICT

Lisa's phone rang an hour later.

"Lisa, what the hell?" fired Jen.

"I'm so sorry, Jen," Lisa said with a touch of defensiveness in her voice.

Jen's voice exploded into the phone. "What. The. Hell?! A retreat. At the parish. Are you kidding me? Seriously?"

"Yeah, it's a silent retreat," Lisa replied gently. "At the Carmelite monastery. It sounds really cool. So I signed up for it. I'm really bummed I don't get to go with you two to the beach. But I'm actually kind of excited about this silent retreat. I've never done anything like this before."

"You signed up for a silent retreat? At a monastery? And you are honestly going to go to that instead of to the beach with your best friends? The ones you have gone to the beach with every year for, what, twenty or thirty years or something? What the hell is the matter with you? *Really?*"

"I really, really feel like God wants me to go on this retreat. It's kind of hard to explain. And, honestly, you haven't been listening to me much lately. I've been thinking about a lot of things in my life."

"You and this thinking thing. You have totally lost your mind. First the tennis tournament. Then you blow me off to go visit some kids' art place. Now this. It's our stinking beach weekend, for God's sake. And you're always talking about strange kinds of stuff now. You're so serious now. Who are you? I do not know who you are. This Lisa, this new thinking Lisa, serious Lisa, I'm not crazy about her. She's selfish. And she's no fun."

"I'm sorry you're disappointed, Jen. You and Amy will have a great time. Y'all will have a blast. I've just been trying to learn what God is up to in my life. I'm in a different place. I guess the dream started it. I'm really not sure. But it feels like something I am supposed to do."

"You're going in some new weird direction. Based on some weird dream. Focusing on weird stuff like death that I don't even want to think about. You're no fun. No tennis. No beach. No room for friends. Do you hear me: You are not fun anymore. You're just weird."

"What are you saying?"

"I'm saying I don't recognize who you are now. And I just can't follow you on this bizarre journey you seem to be on. It's not for me."

Before Lisa could respond, the phone went silent. Jen had hung up.

XXXIV. ANTHONY RETURNS

A week passed. Then another. And before Lisa knew it, she had not seen Anthony for more than a month.

"I've got to see him and tell him all the new things I'm learning," she thought.

So she reached out to see if he had returned from Indianapolis. Finding that he had, she quickly scheduled a coffee.

Lisa greeted Anthony enthusiastically as she helped him into her car to head to the Queen Bee.

"Your list has mesmerized me," she told him. "I hope you had a great visit in Indy."

Anthony beamed. "Wonderful, it was just grand. And to be honest, I've been thinking about my death a lot. And thinking about how I give my life and my love away. Just like I told you."

Lisa nodded. Then Anthony continued, "In fact, I've been ruminating on something for a while. I didn't tell you about it, but it's what inspired me to go to Indy. To spend a month of undivided attention with Teresa and those kids. I had something in mind.

"A while back, I watched one man who knew his cancer only gave him two years to live. He mapped his relationships in four concentric circles: family in the center circle, with his more distant relationships, like business partners, in the outer circle.

"Then he began first to say goodbye and thank you by card or phone call to the people in the outer circles. Next he worked his way to gracefully sunset relationships in person with closer friends and colleagues.

"Finally, with his most treasured relationships in the center circle—a brother, his two closest friends, his wife, his children and his grandchildren—he invested every ounce of life in creating powerful moments of gratitude and blessing in his final months. Uninterrupted. Because he had already said goodbye and thank you to everyone else.

"This man lived another four years instead of two. Probably because he focused his entire life on giving his love away. So, I knew I wanted to be able to do that with Teresa and her kids. Don't get to see them as much since they live farther away. So this trip kind of let me do what that fellow did.

"Thanks for asking. How are you doing? I've been praying for you."

Lisa smiled. "I know. I can feel your prayers all around me. You are so special. Thank you for sharing that with me.

"Your wisdom has set me on a marvelous journey. Still not quite sure where I'm going yet. But I'm learning a lot. I'm even going on a silent retreat this weekend at the Carmelite monastery. And I wanna ask you: Can you please teach me a bit more about this fourth quarter virtue thing? I've really been letting that one simmer in my heart. I'd love to hear more from you if you don't mind."

"That's a good one, isn't it? Glad it got you to thinking," Anthony replied.

"God fertilized the virtue of patience in me as I cared for Mary during her long gradual descent into Alzheimer's. Perhaps that patience really had been in me all my life. Who knows? But God began to draw it out then to grow me in my own fourth quarter.

"I learned to really listen to people. Not merely prepare to respond to them.

"It's why I love being a Saturday Servant. I can visit with those folks for hours on end. They love it. I love it. But I never could have done that earlier in life. No chance. My habit now is to completely listen to those people in the hospital each Saturday when I visit. No distractions. That habit grows patience in my garden and keeps the weeds out.

"And I have watched that patience spill into other parts of my life. Like waiting behind a glacially slow person in the checkout line at the grocery store. I now smile and ask God to fill their life with grace. Because I realize that person may be carrying loads in life I can't even begin to imagine.

"Or when I am sitting in the doctor's office waiting room. And at ninety-seven, I'm there a lot! The wait time can feel like just one more humiliating insult that goes with how my body is betraying me. But this patience now springs up inside me. First, I give thanks that I'm able to go to the doctor. And I've learned to pray silently for each person in that waiting room. I may not know their particular sufferings, but God does. And I want to help.

"You get my point. Focusing on this one virtue injects power into every aspect of your life.

"Like I said before, identify the virtue you believe God has placed in you specifically for your fourth quarter.

"Embrace it.

"Pursue it.

"Pick a habit to fertilize it.

"Then watch that virtue grow.

"You'll be transformed into something even more beautiful than you already are."

part four

METAMORPHOSIS

"Yesterday is gone. Tomorrow has not yet
come. We have only today."

— Mother Teresa

XXXV: ALONE

Lisa packed sparingly for the retreat.

Just one large cloth shopping bag with some light clothes, a prayer journal, a rosary, and a book about Teresa of Avila the nuns had suggested.

She took no makeup. Cell phones and laptops were totally forbidden.

The Carmelites had made it clear: This would be a time for simplicity and placing herself raw before God. No distractions.

Only silence. And listening.

The mere thought of those two words had consumed Lisa for days. She couldn't wait to dive into that deep pool of silence and await whatever God might have in store.

The early-morning, hour-long drive to Our Lady of Mount Carmel Monastery gave Lisa plenty of time to think. The nuns had scheduled the retreat to begin at eight a.m., but she had left her house just after six to be safe. She wanted to give herself plenty of time to make the drive and arrive without rushing. No distractions.

Lisa instinctively knew busyness would be her enemy for these next two days. So she intentionally worked to eliminate any chance the "busy disease" had of infecting her spirit.

She also decided not to listen to music on the traffic-free roads at six on a Saturday morning. Her car remained silent.

Worry knocked at the door of her mind. She tried not to answer.

She then began to wonder if perhaps she had made a mistake. This would be the first time she had ever not gone on the beach getaway with Jen and Amy.

Her decision to say yes to this retreat had meant saying no to sacred time with her dearest friends. And it might even have cost her her friendship with Jen. That hurt.

Lisa had never done anything like this before. A silent retreat. Time away with eleven people she had never even met. In a place she had never visited. She realized she had no idea what Carmelite nuns actually do on a day-to-day basis.

All these unknowns made her stomach twitch. Her mind nervously began to second-guess itself. Maybe she really should have gone on the beach weekend with her girlfriends.

By the time she pulled in to the entrance to the monastery, Lisa recognized a feeling that made her even more uncomfortable. She was alone. Completely.

In the car.

On this retreat.

Away from her friends.

Alone.

For the next thirty-three hours, she would be an island of one in a sea of sheer silence. Joining eleven complete strangers with one common purpose:

To listen for the whisperings of God.

XXXVI. PEACE

Lisa offered a quick prayer to God and a Hail Mary.

Then she got out of her car and walked across the pebble parking lot toward the monastery entrance.

A small sign welcomed her to the retreat. With a brief sentence at the bottom: "From this moment until 5:00 pm on Sunday, please remain silent."

Lisa opened the door and entered the four walls of her silent freedom. For two days, it would be just her and God. Goodbye, world.

The small registration table displayed packets, one for each guest. Lisa found hers and opened it to find a printed agenda, a name tag, and a room assignment.

She walked down the corridor and located her small room. The door was open, her cell carefully prepped by the nuns. As she entered, Lisa saw only a small bed, not much larger than a cot. And a single lamp.

No table. No chair. Just a simple bed and lamp.

She placed her bag on the floor beside the bed and pulled out the agenda. In one hour, the registrants would gather for prayer in the chapel to officially begin the retreat.

The simplicity of the room reminded her of a story Fr. Juan had shared in one of his homilies. About a traveling American who visited a wise Polish rabbi.

The visitor was struck by how bare the rabbi's apartment was.

"Where's your furniture?" she asked the rabbi.

"Where's yours?" the rabbi responded.

"Oh, I am only passing through," the visitor said.

"Me too. I'm only passing through," the rabbi replied.

Then Fr. Juan had said, "Simplicity is your friend. It leads directly to contentment."

"How true that feels right now," Lisa whispered to no one in particular.

Other guests rustled around the hallway, getting settled into their own cells. Lisa wandered down the hall to locate a restroom. Last door on the left. Inside she found a small toilet and sink.

On the short walk back to her cell, she noticed the silence. Everywhere. Like mist enshrouding the mountains on an early morning hike. It simply hung in the air.

Lisa relaxed. She took a deep breath. And embraced her new normal for the next two days. Blissful quiet. Simplicity.

And peace.

XXXVII. PRAYER

After the retreatants had prayed in the chapel in silence for thirty minutes, a nun motioned for the group to follow her into a nearby room.

The guests sat in a semicircle of folding chairs. Eight women and four men.

Before them stood a young nun, wearing the brown Carmelite habit, complete with rosary, scapular and veil. Both her youth and her beauty startled Lisa. She had been expecting a frumpy, elderly sister to lead the retreat. Instead, a slender, fair-skinned woman stood before her, about five feet six with lots of brown hair pinned up inside her veil.

"She looks a lot like me at that age," Lisa reflected.

"I'm Sister Anastasia," the nun began. "And I'll be your informal leader during this silent retreat. My role is pretty minimal, really. You'll be doing most of the work. Silence. Prayer. Listening. You and God.

"I'm simply here to do two main things:

"First, to be sure you have what you need.

"Second, to offer you three short talks. Kind of like mile markers along the path of your journey. A little encouragement for you as you step into the heart of God.

"If you need anything, please know I'm here for you. But you should find everything you need in your packet. Information, suggestions, itinerary, all that stuff.

"In this first time together, I'd like to share a little about silent prayer. Your conversation with God.

"We're Carmelites. You know that. We build much of our life around the wisdom shared with us through great people like Teresa of Ávila, John of the Cross, and Thérèse of Lisieux.

"Solitude and interior prayer. These are the keys for us.

"As you begin these thirty-three hours of silence, I offer three basic thoughts for you to chew on.

"First, Teresa says, 'God does not lead everyone on the same path.'

"That's really good news. There's no need to compare yourself to anyone else on this retreat, or what they are doing or experiencing. You have your own path. With God, for God, and to God. Trust that. This is your journey.

"Second, John says, 'The center of the soul is God.'

"That may jar you a bit. But it can also provide you great comfort. What you are seeking is already with you and in you. It's not out there somewhere. Fear not. It's right here.

"Finally, Carmelites live into the idea that God attracts the soul through love. It really is that simple. Love is the core of everything. It's the sole purpose of us and of all creation.

"Your goal here—and in life really—is to have your soul satisfied in love. Love for God. Love for yourself. And love for the people around you.

"That's all I want to say right now. This is your journey. God lies at the center of your soul. Love will lead you there.

"Please know I'm praying for you. As are all my sisters here. May your journey be saturated in love."

With that, Sister Anastasia pointed the group back to their agenda.

And she left the room.

XXXVIII. PANIC

With Sister Anastasia gone, the room returned to complete silence.

Lisa sat staring squarely into the face of her own restlessness. She had struggled to pay attention even during the few minutes Sr. Anastasia was speaking. No matter how hard she tried, her mind buzzed like a mosquito in perpetual motion.

Worse, she had been distracted by Sr. Anastasia's presence. This young, lovely woman seemed just, well, so calm. So serene.

That serenity rattled Lisa. Mainly because it stood in stark contrast to her own anxiety. And her fear.

Doubts crashed through the door of Lisa's expectations for this retreat. Her hopes of silence and peace collided head-on with the reality of her own busyness and her attachments to friends and financial worries and her own kids.

It seemed like Sr. Anastasia's world looked very unlike her own.

The contrast threw Lisa into near despair.

Negative thoughts and emotions flooded her spirit:

Maybe I am not meant for this kind of thing.

How stupid am I to think I fit in a place like this?

I am so silly. I'm not that spiritual. I'm just a poser, a pretender who wanted to be something I'm not. I go to Mass once a week and take Communion to a few old ladies. That's all.

I've got no business being here.

Lisa could not control the panic. She felt so out of place. And also so alone.

So she did the unthinkable.

The agenda's next block of time simply said: Silent Prayer.

For three hours.

Until lunch time.

Lisa quickly considered her options. And decided to take a walk. To her car.

She combed through the console of the sedan and found her cell phone. She had hidden it there, just in case. She knew the rules, but she also realized the Carmelite sisters did not understand her life. She was a widow. A grandmother. And a real estate agent.

"What do a bunch of Carmelites know about any of that?" she silently insisted.

She had brought the phone, rationalizing that there might be an instance of need. And this panic was it.

She quickly called Amy, at the beach with Jen.

When Amy answered, Lisa almost shouted, "Amy, this is Lisa."

"I know, I could see it on my phone. That's why I answered. Are you OK?"

"Yes ... no ... I mean, I don't know, really. I think I may have made a mistake in coming. I don't think I fit here."

"What's going on?"

"Well, we started with silence. And that was OK. For a little while. But this is a lot of silence. And I'm just not used to that, you know? It's a lot. Like, a whole lot. Like, an ocean of it."

"OK."

"Well, then this nun, Sister Anastasia, gets up. And

she's crazy young. I mean, what does she know about my life? Nothing. She's probably thirty. Like my kids. And she welcomes us to the retreat."

"That sounds really nice. What's the matter?"

"Then she says a few words about prayer. I don't really remember what she said. Love. Stuff like that. It's hard to pay attention in all this silence. I don't know why it makes me so nervous. I just feel so overwhelmed. I'm not sure I'm cut out for this kind of thing."

"Lisa, Lisa, it's OK. It really is. You had a strong sense you should go on this retreat. I'm not sure I understand all that. But you had a really deep conviction. And I believe you're on some sort of journey. It's just a monastery—not some prison. It'll be OK. I mean, how bad can it get?"

"I don't know. I guess I'm just scared."

"You're there for God. That's what you said—that God seems to be telling you something and you want to figure it out. It's just a day and a half. If you hate it, go take a nap or something. But I think you'll really regret it if you don't stick with it and see where it goes."

Lisa took a deep breath. "Thank you. You're probably right. I think I just freaked out. It's just so different from anything I've ever done before."

"You're my friend. I'll always be here for you. Now go do whatever it is you believe God wants you to do. And I'm going back to my beach weekend. We miss you, by the way. We really do."

"Thank you, Amy. I love you. Thank you."

Lisa hung up. And placed the phone back in the console of the car.

She looked around guiltily to see if anyone was watching her.

Then she began to walk calmly through the monastery grounds.

XXXIX. GARDENING

Later that day, Sister Anastasia gathered the silent troops right before dinner.

"I've been praying for you today," she began. "I hope you're entering into the silence without too much turbulence. Sometimes it takes a few hours to settle in. We live in a noisy world that often sounds like wild chimpanzees at the zoo. Most folks don't realize how much noise fills their life until they crash head-on into an immovable wall of stillness."

Lisa nodded in agreement.

"I'd like to share a few thoughts for you to ponder in your prayer time this evening after dinner," the nun continued. "After we eat, we'll meet for prayer in the chapel for an hour. Although you're certainly welcome to stay as long as you like past that. Time in the chapel will help keep you focused."

Sister Anastasia paused. The silence again settled in the room for a moment.

"Now, Teresa compared your soul to a garden. With God at the center of the garden."

These words immediately captured Lisa's imagination. She had been gardening all her life. Some of her favorite moments, whether alone or with her children, had occurred as she sank her fingers into the soil of the garden in her backyard. The connection to the earth. The magic of watching flowers grow from a small seed placed in the dirt. The delight of tomatoes appearing on the vine. The beauty of the roses arranged perfectly by the hand of God.

Lisa listened intently to the sister's instruction.

"Beautiful flowers bloom in your garden. God has placed them there. Those are the virtues: Your generosity. Your patience. The love you display. Your kindness.

"Your role is to water the garden. That's what you seek to do. In fact, that's why you're here. To water your soil.

"Prayer provides the moisture that allows your garden to flourish. Now, Teresa described two primary kinds of prayer. I share them with you for your evening tonight, especially for your hour in the chapel.

"First, meditation.

"You *choose* to do meditation. It requires your intentionality.

"You decide to meditate on something that elevates your soul toward God. Maybe on a verse from Scripture. Or imagining a scene from the life of Jesus. Or a piece of art. Something like that.

"Meditation you can do on your own as you seek the Lord. This effort you give to Him.

"Second, contemplation.

"This prayer arrives as a sheer *gift*. Contemplation. Your deep openness to God. Your welcoming of Him. The yes you often don't even know you are saying. This is more receiving. In a sense, you receive deep prayer. And love.

"Meditation you *offer*. Contemplation you *receive*.

"As Teresa said, 'The important thing is not to think much but to love much.'

"I invite you to spend some of your silence tonight permitting the peace to settle in. Perhaps meditate. And then allow contemplation to open you up to welcome our Lord with open arms.

"The key is love. Let love water your garden."

Lisa relaxed in the folding chair. And she sensed Sister Anastasia's words opening the door of her heart to the possibilities of love.

"I have come to the right place. At the right time," she said to herself. "God really is waiting for me here."

Now she was ready to receive.

And to listen.

XL. ASSUMPTION

Early the next morning, the twelve silent seekers of God attended Mass in the monastery chapel.

Afterward, the silence shared at breakfast now felt normal. Lisa strained to remember any other time in her life when she'd felt so centered and still.

Sister Anastasia motioned for the group to move into the small conference room.

"As Carmelites, we share a deep love and attachment to Mary," she began.

"Mary lives at the center of who we are and what we do.

"You have had a full day of silence. And a good night's rest, I hope.

"And now a new day of quiet and prayer awaits pregnantly before you.

"I'd like to suggest you focus these next hours on Mary.

"For me, personally, her Assumption draws me in. I envision that moment, at the end of her earthly life, as Jesus comes and takes her by the hand to lead her home. To be at His side in heaven. Assumed body and soul into heavenly glory. Isn't that beautiful?

"This marvelous vessel of holiness. She contained the Word of God Himself. And she accompanied Him each step of the way, all the way to the cross. Mary could never be reduced to decay. Jesus would never allow that.

"Mary is very special to me. She mirrors our deepest hopes. She displays the beautiful goal our bodies and souls are destined for: To be with Him. Forever.

"We'll share in Christ's resurrection, just like Mary, our Mother. What confidence that gives us!

"God invites you onto a wonderful journey with Him. Toward Him, actually.

"Such a bold promise. My body and soul in heaven. With my Lord.

"In your prayer time, I invite you to meditate on that.

"Saint Benedict used to say, 'Remember your death each day.'

"You will die.

"You will be judged.

"You will step into something new. You will transition to new life.

"Those who become purified in Christ will ultimately join Him and Mary in Heaven. Body and soul on the Last Day.

"Those who are not, will be condemned. The Church calls that hell.

"Spend some time in silence.

"Invite Mary to help you consider your own death and destiny.

"You know who you are. And you know where you're going.

"Perhaps devote an hour in the chapel later to this. Mary. Jesus. Heaven. These things are true. And real.

"Two questions for you to ponder in your heart as you think about your own death:

1. What matters most in your life now?
2. What matters least?"

Sister Anastasia paused and then smiled.

"I love doing this so much. My sisters here call me

the Nun of Death. I never get tired of dreaming about our destiny. We can be with our Blessed Mother," she said, motioning toward a statue of Mary in the corner of the room.

"And with Him."

She gazed at the crucifix on the wall.

"All joy will enter into us.

"I mean, really, can you imagine anything better?"

XLI. PENETRATION

Sister Anastasia's message pierced Lisa's heart like an arrow of truth.

The invitation to consider her own death triggered her memory of hovering above her funeral and overhearing the haunting words of Christopher:

"Do all parents think they are a nine or a ten? Is that a thing? When really they are just a five or maybe a six?"

But now, rather than recoiling from the sting of those words, Lisa could reflect on what she really wanted her life to be. And how she wanted to love her children and grandchildren.

The silence allowed her to consider things in a fresh way. God did have dreams for her. And she intended to discover them.

Lisa knew she had made the right decision in choosing this retreat. Even if the choice had been painful. Her dream, and her sixtieth birthday, and all the other signs around her had sparked a new journey. One she was fully meant to be on.

Heaven.

Resurrection.

These words reminded Lisa of her priest, who loved to chant, "We are Easter people. We are Easter people."

She eagerly re-entered the silent freedom she had discovered yesterday.

She began to meditate on her own death.

And Mary.

And resurrection.

And heaven.

She had no idea what she might hear from God. But now she knew what she really wanted to ask:

"What matters most?"

Best of all, she knew God would be listening.

XLII. GRATITUDE

At five o'clock that evening, Sister Anastasia herded the twelve retreatants to the front door of the monastery.

"This is it. Our time together has concluded. You are free to leave or to hang around. You may speak or you may continue in silence as long as you like. Your choice.

"Thank you for giving me the sacred privilege of serving you. My prayer for you is that this is not the end. But only the beginning.

"God bless you."

She turned to re-enter the monastery. Lisa quickly tapped her arm and said, "Thank you so much, Sister Anastasia. I am so grateful for this time. God bless you too."

Sister simply nodded and walked through the door, gently closing it behind her.

Lisa sat down on the front steps. Wanting to savor the sweet taste of this retreat just a little while longer.

She gave thanks to God. For the retreat. For Sister Anastasia and her Carmelite sisters. For His goodness. For the dreams He had for her. For the promises embodied in Mary. For His love. For all of it.

A few minutes passed. Lisa stood and slowly walked toward her car.

It was time to begin heading home.

In more ways than one.

XLIII. GRATITUDE DEUX

Lisa eased her car slowly out of the monastery parking lot. Her heart yearned to linger. Afterglow, they call it.

Beginning the hour-long drive home, she called her friend.

"How's the beach?"

"It's just wonderful," Amy replied. "I really wish you were here. Jen just left to head back home."

"Well, I'm so glad you have some time there by yourself. Just to enjoy the beauty. And the peace and quiet," Lisa said.

"Me too. How was the retreat? Did you end up staying for the whole thing?" Amy asked.

"Yes. And I'm so glad I did."

"Tell me all about it. I was worried about you after that panicky phone call. How did it go?"

"It's almost too much for me to share right now. It was just so wonderful. How about we grab a glass of wine when you get back and I'll fill you in on the details then? Right now, I really just wanted to call and say thank you."

"Thank you for what?" Amy asked.

"Thank you for being a supportive friend. I'm really, really grateful. Even when you didn't completely understand what was going on, you were still on my side. And I appreciate that. So, thank you."

"We're friends, Lisa. That's what friends do."

"I know. But I wanted to say it anyway. I love you. And I look forward to sharing with you some more in a week or two. I probably need that long just to digest everything from the past two days anyway. It really was wonderful. Enjoy the beach and we'll talk soon."

"Thank you. I hear the joy in your voice. I can't wait to see you."

XLIV. PROGRESS

The fall turned into winter.

Lisa snuck in the side door and slipped into a seat near the back of the classroom.

A woman stood in front, demonstrating how to turn clay on a potter's wheel for a group of awestruck children. The wheel's hum mesmerized the kids as they watched small flecks of clay being flung into the air.

The potter led the children one by one to the front to touch the clay. Their faces radiated as if they were looking at a sparkling tree surrounded with toys on Christmas morning.

When the potter's presentation ended, Lisa guided the class of third graders through the studios at Playful Possibilities. In one, they paused to watch a woman painting a still life from a bowl of fruit sitting on the table before her.

Like a caring shepherd, Lisa then directed the students into a sculptor's space. A disheveled man stood gazing at a large piece of marble, envisioning what could be. He carefully marked key points on the stone with chalk. The students joked about what they could do with a chisel and hammer.

Playful Possibilities housed spaces for all kinds of artistic expressions. From photography to music, the latter being a single small room with a piano where a musician occasionally stopped by to practice or perform for the children.

At the end of the tour, a small band of volunteers greeted Lisa and the children with refreshments. The large gathering space in the center of the facility showcased varieties of art produced by the local talent. Even one large bird made from colorful fabrics descended from the ceiling as if it were about to land on the children's heads.

Smiles abounded. Including the one on Lisa's face.

She had found herself smiling a lot ever since she had begun spending her Tuesdays at Playful Possibilities shortly after her silent retreat. Another step in her plan to follow the quiet voice of God inviting her into a new chapter.

The art inspired her. The artists encouraged her.

Lisa had begun to rediscover her love for sketching and drawing. And now she yearned to learn to paint.

Tuesdays had become Lisa's favorite day of the week.

XLV. CHALLENGES

Playful Possibilities had opened up a new window for Lisa. And the light shining through that window infused her days with optimism.

But spiritually, she found herself struggling with forgiveness.

For eight years, she had not really been paying attention to a nagging resentment she felt toward Brian. She had loved him, to be sure. But the gaping failure to prepare for his own death lingered in her heart. Thinking of the mess of unknowns he had left her still made her anxious. And a touch of bitterness reminded her that his lack of real emotional investment and his half-hearted support of her faith clung to her soul like barnacles on the hull of a ship.

Lisa knew Anthony was right. She needed to find a way to forgive. To set herself free from the poison within her.

"Life is short," she told herself. "Brian is dead. It's time to move forward."

She had long ago learned to accept Brian's gaps. She knew she herself was not perfect, so it was unfair to expect him to be. She navigated around his weaknesses and found ways to celebrate his very real strengths.

She had found comfort over the years by offering Brian's meager faith up to the heart of Jesus. Deep down, she knew she would not be able to change him. And frankly, it wasn't her job to transform him. It was her job merely to love him. And she had done that well.

God had made Brian, so she had left him in the capable hands of Jesus decades ago. Contentment slowly replaced her frustration because she knew God would be at work in ways she could not.

Now Lisa wanted to learn to fully forgive her husband. A fork in the road appeared before her. One path leading to thriving. The other to merely surviving.

She didn't want to waste energy carrying the baggage of old wounds into this new phase of her journey.

Lisa also realized she needed to forgive Jen for her rejection and release that burden as well. They might not become friends again, but the pain of that loss did not need to poison her own garden.

Sister Anastasia's words echoed down the hallways of Lisa's memory: "Your soul is like a garden. With God at the center."

"That's more true than I ever knew," Lisa thought to herself.

"This fourth quarter living is like my rose garden. Some planning. Some hard work. A few thorns. Some beautiful blossoms and flowers. A touch of rain. And a little bit of magic wonder mixed in to stimulate the growth."

She chuckled. Roses bloom only when the gardener embraces the right habits.

XLVI. COURAGE

Early on Saturday morning, Lisa took her place in the long line at the parish.

"Why does the parish only offer confession at this ungodly hour?" she asked herself. "Does anyone really get up at seven a.m., eager to release some bitterness?"

The number of people waiting for confession surprised her. Then again, it had been a long while since she had partaken of this sacrament herself.

She fidgeted like a chain-smoker. Nervous because it had been so long.

"How long has it been? A year? No ... three, maybe? Yikes!" she thought.

Lisa stared at her shoes. A bit embarrassed to be seen by folks she recognized and knew. She hoped they couldn't read the list of failures and wounds forming in her mind's notepad.

She called to mind the calming truth of Anthony: Forgive. Often.

By now, Anthony's wisdom, Sister Anastasia's insights, and Amy's encouragement had formed a trifecta of healthy voices in her mind. Lisa liked to call them the "committee in my head." They served together like her own team of fourth quarter spiritual cheerleaders.

The line drew nearer to the doorway to mercy. Lisa collected her thoughts. She wanted to be sure to cover two things with Fr. Juan.

First, forgiving Brian. To ask God to forgive her for hanging on to resentment for so long. How much time and energy had she wasted nursing those almost ancient hurts anyway?

Second, forgiving Jen. Her long-time friend clearly didn't understand what God was up to in all this. And Lisa knew she shouldn't blame Jen for being in a different place on the journey than she herself was. Clinging to anger at Jen's harsh rejection served no one. Time to let it go. And ask God to heal them both.

Finally, the door opened. A tall man stepped out, placed his cap on his head and moved toward the exit.

Lisa entered the small room. She knelt by the

screen. Crossed herself. And began to speak the words of hope.

"Father, forgive me ..."

XLVII. LUNCH

The table in the front window at the Bistro maintained its power to always feel familiar and comfortable.

Lisa and Amy ordered glasses of white wine. Chardonnay for Lisa. Riesling for Amy. The usual.

"You look fantastic! You really do," Amy said with a sparkle in her eye.

"Thank you, my dear friend. You look pretty darn good your own self," replied Lisa warmly.

"It's been, like, forever since I saw you. I'm so sorry. Life kind of got away from me after I got back from the beach. Daniel's business has gotten crazy! And he's needing me to do all kinds of stuff I haven't done before—place orders, organize payroll, blah blah blah. So ... how you been?"

Lisa smiled. "I'm actually doing really, really well. Like my aunt Helen used to say, 'I'm pleased as punch!'"

"OK, girl," Amy replied. "Tell me all about it."

"Well, like I told you, the retreat went really well. It

was a great next step in my life. You know I had been percolating for a while on that dream of my death and funeral. And really trying to digest what Kevin and Anthony had said about my fourth quarter."

"Right."

"The retreat just kind of brought everything together in a wonderful way. The silence was rich. Wow, Amy, you really should try that sometime. It's powerful."

"I've heard that. No pun intended." Amy stopped and chuckled at herself before continuing.

"So I did try to welcome the silence at the beach when I had the place to myself for a few days after Jen left. I have to admit, the weight of that silence really surprised me. Maybe you're teaching me a thing or two here also."

"Good for you. How is Jen, by the way?" Lisa asked. " I haven't heard from her."

"She's doing OK. Seems kind of agitated lately. Not sure if it's her daughter. Or the thing with you. Or something else. She hasn't really opened up about it."

"I miss her. I hope one day we'll be able to repair

our relationship. But, either way, I have forgiven her. I realized I need to let her be on her own journey. That's OK. And she doesn't have to understand mine ... Anyway, back to the retreat. This beautiful young nun, Sister Anastasia, hosted us. I'm not sure she's even thirty. But boy, does she get it. She gave us three short talks on prayer. Very short. But very deep. She said the most beautiful things about Mary and death. And resurrection."

Amy nodded. "That's great. So ... how has your life been since the retreat?"

"Peaceful ... Yeah, I think that's the word. And joyful."

"Wow, Lisa. I'm just so happy for you. Good for you!"

"Yeah, thanks. I've really been trying to dream about what lies ahead. In this life. And in the next. You know?"

Amy hesitated a bit, not sure what to say about such a delicate topic.

Lisa sensed her friend's struggling. "I guess I've never really thought much about what comes next.

Sister Anastasia said something like 'Remember your death daily.' That kind of stuck with me.

"I know now that I'm going to die. That dream I had reminded me of that. But the truth of it really sank in deeply at the retreat.

"And I want to be ready.

"I want to live this next season well. It's my final chapter, you know? And I want to be ready to transition into the next life. It's actually kind of exciting to think about. Really helps me get clear about what matters most in my life. And what matters least."

Amy listened attentively.

She nodded and told Lisa, "You're reminding me of that old bawdy romance novel writer. I think her name was Shirley. She said, 'First things first; second things never.'"

Lisa laughed.

Then Amy said, "Thank you for sharing this with me. You've had quite an experience. Several, really. Ones I haven't had. But now you're making me kind of hope I will. You're discovering something I think I probably need to learn."

"Well, I don't know about that. But I do know this: I want to live the rest of my life with no regrets. And I'm sure gonna try to figure out how."

XLVIII. JOY

Art and children. The positivity of Tuesdays watered a seed Lisa had forgotten lived within her.

So much so that she decided to explore Playful Possibilities twice a week instead of just once.

Tuesdays, to lead the children into a world of beauty and inspiration.

And Thursdays, to work on her own art.

With the help of an encouraging painter named Nicholas, Lisa applied her drawing skills to learn to paint with watercolors. She set up a small easel and supplies near Nicholas's space. He coached her first in the basics of painting a simple rose resting on the table.

As he guided her, Lisa felt like she was in grade school again, discovering artistic wonders for the very first time. Using a brush, finding the right color combinations, setting the proportions onto the paper—all of these challenged Lisa in new ways. She relished the adventure of it all. On Thursdays, she wore a smile.

Week by week, month by month, Lisa grew and developed.

At times, she found her mind wandering.

"Why have I never thought of trying this before?

"Why have I let these artistic instincts lie dormant for oh so many years?"

But, when doubts crept in, she remembered Anthony's coaching: Maybe God really had placed these gifts of art deep within her for this very moment.

With each passing month, she recognized something blossoming in her soul.

She named it for what it was: Joy.

A virtue.

A beautiful virtue.

Joy.

In his fourth quarter, Anthony had embraced the virtue of patience. Agnes, the nurse, had welcomed fortitude. And Arthur had focused on wisdom as he transitioned from executive to mentor.

"Maybe, just maybe," Lisa said to herself, "Joy will be my own fourth quarter virtue. The one God uses to paint a masterpiece in me."

part five

AFTERWORD
(Nineteen Years Later)

"You are what you love."

— Augustine

AFTERWORD

Raindrops pattered lightly on umbrellas as the crowd filed into Sacred Heart parish.

Amy and Daniel struggled to find a seat. Traffic had them running late, but they were not going to miss this moment for anything.

By the time they arrived, Sacred Heart was nearly full. Organ music lifted gently through the rafters and echoed off the stained glass windows.

Children—some accompanied by parents, some by chaperoning artists—filled an entire section of the church.

At last, Lisa's family began to process down the center aisle, led by Sacred Heart's new pastor, Fr. Richard. He had come to the parish just last year.

The family members made their way to the six pews reserved at the front of the church.

Michael, his wife, Susan, and their three children led the family members.

Emily and her husband, Ron, followed. As did Noah,

Lisa's first grandchild, who was now in college. Tall and angular, Noah received admiring smiles from his younger siblings as they took their seats.

Christopher was next. Now married, with two children of his own. Lisa's youngest child clasped notes in his hand as he and his family entered the third pew.

Lisa's siblings sat together. Filling two and a half pews by themselves with their spouses and most of Lisa's nephews and nieces.

With so many children in attendance, the Mass sounded more like a street festival than a funeral. An occasional spontaneous shout. A "shhhsh" from a scolding parent. And loud clapping, accompanying a song requested by Lisa for use at the start of the Mass.

Joy had arrived confidently and swept out any speck of sadness lingering in the church.

Once the Mass concluded, Fr. Richard invited Christopher to speak on behalf of the family. Proudly standing before the assembly of friends, family and children, Christopher began.

"Like you, I loved my mother. Maybe she was your friend, or your mentor at Playful Possibilities, or your teammate in taking Communion to parishioners on Saturdays. However you knew her, I am so glad you're here.

"'Lisa.' It means 'devoted to God.' The name just fit her, didn't it?

"We're celebrating Mom's life. Grieving her death, yes. But, most of all, giving thanks for her transition to new life. As she battled cancer these past few years, she always liked to smile and say, 'We are Easter people.' Then she would say something about Sister Anastasia, the Nun of Death, her dear friend. I see you there, Sister. Thank you so much for being here. Mom really enjoyed corresponding with you over these past, what, twenty years or so?"

Everyone in the church turned to look at Sister Anastasia, who was clearly uncomfortable with this kind of public attention.

Christopher continued. "Anyway, so many of you have been touched by Mom's kindness. Her generosity. Her love. She really was a ten out of ten, wasn't she?"

He paused.

"Something happened to her years ago that generated an enormous energy in her life. When she turned sixty, lots of stuff—a dream, a retreat, conversations with some of you—sparked Mom to focus on a few specific things in what she liked to call her 'fourth quarter.' She discovered the five keys to living and dying with no regrets.

"I bet you received these five keys from her. Little No Regrets cards she had made by an artist friend at his print shop. I brought some to share with you today as you leave.

"Mom inserted these cards, like sacred tablets, in her Christmas letters to people she loved. Said this truth was just too good not to share.

"Her passion exploded. And filled every aspect of her life. And to be honest, Mom really inspired me. You too, I imagine.

"She rediscovered her love for art, then began sharing that passion with so many children. It startles me to see so many of you kids here today all in one place. To think you loved my mom like I did really warms my heart. I'm so glad you're here.

"And she encountered other artists—thank you, Frank and Nicholas, for helping her learn to paint, first with watercolors, and then with acrylics. She just loved that. My house is filled with her paintings now."

Christopher stopped. Took a deep breath. Swallowed hard.

His voice hesitated.

"Most of all, she grew in faith. So many of you played a role in that. Hasn't it been fun to watch her dig deep into the soil of her own soul and grow into such a remarkably loving woman? Her prayer life blossomed; she'd just sit in the silence of her rose garden and spend what seemed like hours bathing in the presence of God. And His love.

"Love.

"She loved us kids. And especially her grandkids. Oh my gosh!

"Over these past twenty years, she made it a point to spend at least one week at each of our homes every year. Just giving us all of her undivided attention, and love.

"Mom really had thought a lot about her death. And

that stimulated so much of how she lived her fourth quarter. Her motto was very simple: 'Full of joy. No regrets.'

"She wanted to pour it all out—all her life, all her love—into her family, her parish, and the people around you here today. It was beautiful to observe.

"I will always remember the last words she said to me, as she lay dying in hospice. 'You have been such a wonderful son.' In those last moments, she didn't speak about herself. Instead, she said what I needed to hear.

"I will miss Mom, no question. You will too. But something much larger is happening here.

"My mother, Lisa, grew in joy—that centerpiece of her final years. My mom, through her habits, and her passion, became a person of joy. In every way.

"In the end, she died well. And she lived even better.

"So today we celebrate that. For her, this moment, her funeral Mass, is not the end at all. It's just the beginning."

appendix

NEXT STEPS

"A man is not old until
regrets take the place of dreams."

— John Barrymore

NEXT STEPS

Now that you have begun this journey, we offer you some next steps to continue dreaming about the possibilities for your own fourth quarter.

Be ready.

There is no time like the present to begin envisioning how you will live and die with no regrets.

A sense of urgency will fuel you.

Tragically, most people become used to living without urgency.

And complacency sets in.

If you are complacent about your life, you will be complacent about your friendships.

If you are complacent about your life, you will be complacent about your work.

If you are complacent about your life, you will be complacent about your marriage.

If you are complacent about your life, you will settle for anything.

You will stop dreaming.

And when there is no dream for life, you will not attach to any other dream.

Complacency bleeds into everything.

So, be ready.

There is no time like the present.

To assist you, we have created a unique workbook with powerful exercises specifically designed to help you pray, imagine, and dream. Through these exercises, you will begin to map a clear path to maximize the five keys to living and dying with no regrets. Whether you are already in your fourth quarter, or are just beginning to consider what yours might look like, the workbook will inspire your plan with hope.

The 5 Keys to Living and Dying with No Regrets

Say Yes to God
God invites you onto a wonderful journey.
When you say yes to God's invitation,
you know where you're going.

Focus on a Fourth Quarter Virtue
Pursue one fourth quarter virtue God has specifically
placed in you. Then watch it create blossoms in all
areas of your life.

Give. It. Away.
The more you give yourself away,
the happier you'll be.

Forgive. Often.
Bitter and resentful is no way to live.
And it's definitely no way to die.

Be Open to Life
Your fourth quarter can be more of a birthing than a
dying. Be open to what can be.

15 Beautiful Virtues:

1. Courage
2. Prudence
3. Faith
4. Hope
5. Love
6. Justice
7. Joy
8. Peace
9. Patience
10. Kindness
11. Generosity
12. Faithfulness
13. Gentleness
14. Self-Control
15. Humility

"Since we are travelers and pilgrims in this world,
let us think upon the end of the road,
that is of our life,
for the end of our way is our home ...
Let us not love the road rather than our home ...
Let us know that although we are strangers to the
Lord while in the body,
we are present to the eyes of God."

- Saint Columban